D1232609

Why so much fear of tears? Because the masks we use are made of salt. A stinging, red salt which makes us beautiful and majestic but devours our skin.

Luisa Valenzuela

OTHER TITLES IN THE ***MASKS*** SERIES

Leslie Dick ***Without Falling***
Juan Goytisolo ***Landscapes After the Battle***
Luisa Valenzuela ***The Lizard's Tail***

OTHER TITLES FROM ***SERPENT'S TAIL***

Jorge Amado ***Dona Flor and Her Two Husbands***
David Bradley ***The Chaneysville Incident***
Michel del Castillo ***The Disinherited***
Andrée Chedid ***From Sleep Unbound***
Andrée Chedid ***The Sixth Day***
Waguih Ghali ***Beer in the Snooker Club***
Oscar Hijuelos ***Our House in the Last World***
Ismail Kadare ***Chronicle in Stone***
Klaus Mann ***The Turning Point***
Dea Trier Mørch ***Winter's Child***
J.J. Phillips ***Mojo Hand***
Tom Wakefield ***Forties' Child***

THE CRYPTO-AMNESIA CLUB

THE CRYPTO-AMNESIA CLUB

MICHAEL BRACEWELL

The publishers thank Kathy Acker, Mark Ainley, Martin Chalmers, Bob Lumley, Enrico Palandri, Kate Pullinger for their advice and assistance.

British Library Cataloguing in Publication Data
Bracewell, Michael
The crypto-amnesia club.
I. Title
823'.914[F] PR6052.R23
ISBN 1-85242-115-0

First published 1988 by
Serpent's Tail, 27 Montpelier Grove, London NW5

Phototypeset by AKM Associates (UK) Ltd.
Ajmal House, Hayes Road, Southall, London

Printed in Great Britain by
WBC (Print) Bristol Ltd.

An undistinguishable world to men,
The slaves unrespited of low pursuits,
Living amid the same perpetual flow
Of trivial objects, melted and reduced
To one identity, by differences
That have no law, no meaning, and no end –

Wordsworth *The Prelude*: Book VII, Residence in London

For Roger Poole

CONTENTS

ONE

The Crypto-Amnesia Club

These days it always feels like the beginning of the end. I am continually introducing myself — only to go away almost immediately, embarrassed by my rash impulse. The glorious inspiration that I believe I may have touched on one moment all too often reveals itself anew as a rather amateur enthusiasm the next. I never really know where I am. And this is why I think it would be best for me to make my occupation fully known right from the outset; for it is not a good thing, my occupation, and I would rather that you know why. And I would rather that you know why because I am afraid. I am afraid of everything — I am even afraid of you, even from this distance. The mere possibility of your presence is enough to make my knuckles go white, my eyes dart warily from one corner of the room to the other, and my hand roam secretly towards the alarm that I have hidden beneath this desk and which would call someone in to have you thrown out into the street.

I must have had a miserable childhood — I can't remember — but somewhere, surely, in my miserable life, I must have done something good. These days I doubt it. This place feels like the service lift to purgatory, so full of ghosts and the ends of trailing cables, and at the bottom of the shaft is an emotional minefield, the walls splattered with the remains of the imprudently drunk.

So I shall introduce myself, and you will know from the chill on my breath that something is wrong. You will maybe even guess that I live in a place where Nancy would be given a push in the back, down the steps into the cold black river, all scummy with fresh wood shavings. You may tell that I know a bit more than most about why old Bill Sykes took to the rope . . .

I am the reluctant manager of The Crypto-Amnesia Club, a forum, bar, dance hall, living hell — call it what you will. I took over the club quite a while ago and I hate it already. I hate what it does to people, or brings out in people, or in some ways speeds up and crystallizes in people: a horrific doubt on the pinnacle of their idea of themselves, a terrifying view as reward for having clambered up those shifting escarpments of the self-image just to take a look. It's got to me now, as well as the inmates of the club, and I always thought that the boss was immune. Hence my fear.

Last October we had the telephone booths at the club quilted in scarlet plastic. Asylum Chic. What with the flick knife engravings ('Babylon Sunsets'), and people crying in them, people being sick in them, people taking oral in them, people using them as offices, and places to commit suicide or get junked up, this seemed best. Plastic is cheap, it cleans easily, and (if you are regular with your payments) the specialist phone company that deals in this kind of thing will liaise you with a kiosk consultant — some little know-it-all from the London School of Gestural Awareness who is up to date on the semiology of enclosed communication areas — and ensure that your finger remains firmly on the irregular pulse of phone psychology. Since last October I have been paying a lot of money for this service, but can no longer feel the promised pulse. It must have died — like everything else round here.

But phone-awareness is vital in a club like mine. My guests (pigs, snakes and creeps) are choosy about the booth. They look on phones in a personal way. They have the sensitivity of artists when it comes to the blower. Fights start over phones. Phones are tribal to them, my guests, the people who pay the rent. Even if it is just to tell their best-friend-Helen that the cat has massacred another magpie in the garden, the call must be made. And I must cater to the whims of my guests. It's what I'm paid for. So if the Phone Corridor does look like a vorticist painting made entirely out of crashed cars, it's not my fault — directly.

It was a beautiful October day when Lisa from Phone Cell put me wise to phone-psychology, and shattered the peace of my pre-opening drink with the assurance that I was surrounded by potential phono-paths and really ought to consider replacing the down-market, emotionally offensive, wall-hung digitals with something a little more baroque. 'A phone that really says something,' she finished professionally, quoting the script off her sales card with a wooden insincerity that made one blush to be a consumer.

I recognized Lisa from a magazine: a glossy tabloid whose publisher it was impossible to trace to an address more specific than Europe, and whose theme was telephonic fetish. In the usual plastic leisure suit that the Fetish photographers insist all their scenario-participants should wear, Lisa had been gently lashing a complicit schoolgirl who was bondaged with extension cords and abusing herself with a linear receiver. That was where I had last seen Lisa, but now she looked so respectable. So she had cleaned up her act had she? Or was it just an upgrade to telepimping, getting me to pay for my guests to be able to score their own tricks? You slag, Lisa, I thought, it's you that needs help.

The Achilles heel of the drunken rioting slobs who come to my club is isolation. They are all terrified of being alone — even when they are in a crowd. They see the crowd as an individual, that is, they see themselves as a lighthouse, cut off in a lonely sea. They have to be able to contact, to check in — they are permanently adrift. With the help of Phone Cell we developed the Phone Corridor, its walls collaged in raven blue leather to offset the scarlet plastic quilting of the booths. We had floor level strip lighting, and inset TV screens to monitor the activities of in-booth guests for the benefit of voyeurism-friendly clients who could then watch the goings-on on the video screen above the new bar, specially created for that purpose. The use of this annex was an additional charge on the membership fee but it seemed to work, and we made a lot of money.

The technology of the Phone Corridor was wittily top heavy and created by a team of dedicated Japanese softwear sculptors who in turn sub-contracted the lighting installations to Signa Vagabonde of Milan: a hard-hitting crew of filament-surrealists whose speciality was heat-seeking phase bulbs, an invisible arrangement of sensors that would throw a light of any colour at random across anything warm within range. The subtlety of the system lay in the unusual places in which the sensors were installed, and the resultant chaos of luminescence transformed the crowd into what they called Random Human Graffiti. I have even been approached by various eager young film makers whose ambition it is to use our Phone Corridor as a set for their inevitable interpretations of the decadent end of popular fiction, but I refuse to allow it. I explained to the first young director that The Crypto-Amnesia Club was one of the main reasons why people stopped going to the cinema but he was a rank-amateur art leech and didn't understand. I then told him that he could hire the premises for a quarter of a million pounds a week, which soon got rid of him. (He subsequently tried to plagiarise our decor-system by way of a satirical copy, so I sued his company for far more than a quarter of a million pounds and put the story into all the papers: 'TOP PEOPLE'S PUNK CLUB BLOWS FUSE ON FILM THIEF'. Our applications for membership doubled overnight.) So I have made a lot of money out of my guests' fear of isolation, and I feel that I am entitled to every penny of it.

By two in the morning we are generally packed, and the bar

looks like a cross between the Harrod's sale and a Viking funeral. People queue for phones, making good use of their additional membership fee and going pullman class all the way to total oblivion. They must be terrified of missing something. Two girls can generally be found deep in each other's arms in a particular chair that they pay to reserve nightly. Nobody knows who they are, but then nobody cares either.

My head bouncer (or 'Security Artiste' as he prefers to be known) gave his previous occupation as last of the mohicans but didn't name the salary. He does very well out of me however, and for my part I can at least rest safe in the knowledge that no fights will break out as long as he, Sydney, is making the club a little darker and a little colder with his shadow.

We are administratively sound. If you have never seen the paperwork for chaos before, you can take it from me that we have files on everything — from the telephone receipts to the quarantine certificate of our club cat, a persian blue called Amphetamine Psychosis, Amphe for short. Most of the time Amphe is curled up on the desk in my office. My office is the only quiet room in the place, and this is due largely to the soundproofing on the double doors and to my mood. The snakes and spiders out there don't seem to realise that this is *my* wilderness that they're exploiting. I am a reluctant club manager. I am an invisible ring master tracing patterns in the sawdust with my toe and going slowly mad within this sanctum of the top.

I keep tropical fish in a long tank down one wall of my office. They move gently around the shadows and the weeds, teasing themselves on the fine streams of silver bubbles that continually rise through the water. Amphe pays no attention to them whatsoever, too proud of her blue fur to waste time over fish. I have fresh flowers on my desk — freesias and daffodils — and I don't like visitors. Since we really got established I haven't needed to go into the club that much, but I still do, at twelve and three, like a monk to chapel. I still feel some ghastly responsibility for the madness out there, for all those telephone numbers pinned like poems on the walls of old Bedlam next to the Fleet, for all those visitors' signatures: Fawkes, Guido, and Bates. I used to care about the guests, and then I didn't care about them, and now I'm simply cold. It's like watching a film from behind the screen. It's like deep sea diving.

In these troubled times I wake up with the taste of the previous night in my mouth. Its colour fills the office. If I haven't been to bed then I wake to find myself stiff in my desk chair, the low blue lights still burning, and the fish patrolling up and down above the scarlet gravel in their tank. A creased suit walking very slowly across a darkened room at noon to raise a blind and wince at the light is a truly pathetic sight. But I do not claim to know — or even care — about what obscure arrangements a man can come to with his notion of fate or circumstances, which motivates him to act in a particular way. I do know however that there are some men who go way over the agreed overdraft limit that fortune has somehow imposed upon their account. I am such a man. I feel that I have used up all the credit that exists within a life to finance the spirit. It is a fact — sad or otherwise — than when a man becomes bankrupt in this way, not through ill-fortune, or some misplaced yet heroic gamble, but simply through sheer extravagance in the face of a life that makes no sense, then within a second he is left with little more than memories. I have become one of London's overdrawn, my only remaining dignity is that I am fully aware of the fact. Recording this spiritual poverty brings into relief the cheapness of drawing upon the unfunded self, of using sentiments that have neither the prosperous glow of a good return on investment, nor the boyishly handsome youth of a working asset. I have burnt down my listening bank, and it is when the morning dew is glistening on the charred remains that I most feel the loss. My spirit is as wrecked as the old Thames Dockland, but somewhere between the Cuckold's Point and the Devil's Tavern is the enterprise zone of my heart, wherein I cherish my micro-cassette recorder, the playback unit of all my memories. I sit alone in this office, dreaming of shredded cars beside the golden river, tired of living and scared of dying, but that's my problem.

People say 'Why is it called "The Crypto-Amnesia Club"?,' and I think that the answer is in something that Lisa once said: 'People come here to forget but can't quite, and end up remembering something else.' But now I seem to remember everything, and that's why I'm the boss. I understand memory.

Running a club like this makes you sexist — you see so many people existing for sex, and when I look around and see all the painful flesh wounds that the place somewhow inspires, I wonder I continue. I avoid any sexual contact with the guests. I don't want their love, I do this for money.

Sometimes I see myself trapped in this office, calm to the last, surrounded by rotting fruit. Maybe this is why I tour the club at twelve and three, just to make sure that there is no sign of a mutiny. And that is when I really see my guests — the violets and the vandals, the Belle and the Bêtise, the people who put the antic into romanticism. One evening I found a note pinned to my door with a knife, it read: 'Lovers are like Bullets — you never hear the one that gets you.' It was terribly quiet that night.

I am the only person in The Crypto-Amnesia Club who can remember everything. I remember the faces of all the slugs and lizards who bask in the pale pink light of the dancefloor, waves of shifting faces never bored by calculating their next exclamation of the obvious. Such arrogance they have in the face of ideas. I am haunted by those faces although I tell myself a thousand times a night not to believe in them any more than in the minds that they represent.

But it is no use. The memories are getting to me now; all the time. I wonder if there was life before night clubs? Some simple existence with no strings attached? I cannot believe this somehow. I have already rejected this thought as too naive. Maybe I am a recent model on the evolutionary scale: Memory Man. A distinct advance on the Homo Narcissisus and Alcoholic Man who are the wonders of the plasma that come here to dance. But this speculation is useless, and there is still the problem of Lisa from Phone Cell, the girl that I can't help being hopelessly in love with.

'Je t'aime' is French for 'I'm stupid', and I fell in love with Lisa whilst she was working on our Phone Corridor contract. I don't know why I fell in love with her. I scrabbled around hopelessly for something to hold on to as I fell deeper and deeper in love with her. I remember quite clearly the night that I knew I was in love with her for she was due at a meeting in my office and my fear of getting involved with her was bringing on hallucinations. I thought I saw a pre-Lisa age, in which blue fields lay sprinkled with poppies; a meadow before the freeze-up, the terrible glaciation of the spirit upon which this club is built. I saw an asexual age in a landscape with no flesh tones. It seemed as though I had been there for hours in the sunlight, lulled by the silence into a state of pure calm. And then the sky reddened, the sun blushing for the future as it began to set. The ensuing night would incubate horrors: mirrors, telephones, synthetics, nightclubs, and I would somehow get sold (or buy myself) into the late-night entertainment business. I would never be able to benefit from the glorious remorse, confession, repentance and absolution of a spiritual hangover of theologically complex proportions. Let us say that I knew these things because I knew that Lisa was to be the lock and the key of my prison. As an agent of Chaos (being the representative for Phone Cell — a monument to all that I find horrific about The Crypto-Amnesia Club), it was disaster for me to love her. I was trapped in love with all that I fear most. I was in love with a creator of my confinement — no escape.

And then Lisa came into the office. 'Hello,' she said tenderly, 'I thought they'd killed you off.'

The secret of dealing with Lisa is to be certain of no certainties. She lay her long gloves on the desk like a challenge. I moved them back to her side. I was accepting no invitations to test Lisa's total exclusion zone. She smiled slightly at this stock defensive gesture, and I knew that somewhere in the blue darkness of the office the flowers had shuddered.

'I see that you've kept this rat hole well stocked,' she cooed.

'It's the cheese we use,' I replied, loving her more each second. As we sat there testing each other in the darkness, I felt my life flashing before my eyes, more deafening than the Pearl & Dean. Down the catwalk of my tired mind the parade of memories stalked, shimmering into a golden horseshoe of applauding guests, envious colleagues, breath-taken virgins and frantic photographers, all attended by their many assistants. Flash, flash, flash and oh!, the confident smiles of my memory models, really wide: the perfect unobtainable to the muffled thump zoom pow of a Crypto-Amnesia Dub Creation Soundtrack. Nothing will ever be as good as this again.

'Why don't you, why don't you, why don't you come back to my flat?' sighed Lisa in a voice you could pour on a waffle.

'You might murder me,' I replied.

'But I won't,' she whispered, 'honestly, I won't.' And as the blue light fell across her smile I believed her. That night we left the club together, and I don't suppose that anyone saw the way she kissed me beneath the Citicorp Building.

Before her modelling days, perhaps Lisa had been a schoolgirl sunbathing in her parents' garden, and then a resting actress, and then an auditioning glamour girl. Maybe she had stared through her rivals and into the winter sunset thinking, 'Please God, don't ever let me be like them . . .' She did it for money, not for love. And so Lisa came into my life and gave me a reason for living for four months before going away again. That's the way of these things I suppose but I am obessed by the memory of her and by the hope of one day seeing her again.

I have chased these memories around the wet ring roads at night; a fury of possibilities getting caught in multiple pile-ups at the terrible intersections. I have thought of her in all those places that provoke great attempts at resolution by their desperate loneliness. Places like The Vault by Southwark cathedral I have thought of her, and places like the great river Thames I have thought of her, just where Elizabeth and Leicester beat oars and not far from where the Palace beat Spurs.

So I still love Lisa, although I never see her these days, and I don't suppose that she knows how much I suffer for my love of her. She is out there tonight sleeping I suppose, beneath the great expensive moon that is hanging high over the city, whilst I am playing with memories — the executive toys of the broke. Despite being bankrupt I have formed a merger with the night to search for the truth in these memories. We are a young company, but full of ideas, and as we stand here together (the night and I), staring at the end of a snapped golden string, I can feel the cold wind blowing up from the river and hear the passing of late trains into Cannon Street station.

My name is Mr Merril — or simply Merril — I am thirty-three years old, and I am the manager of The Crypto-Amnesia Club.

TWO

Britannia

My crypto-anmnesia:
Despise participation, and *emptiness* will come from within and without. When a mind is received into *emptiness* (as mine so frequently is), the body becomes complicit. Moments of beauty — or of inspiration — are born out of, and witnessed in, solitude. The office. Love becomes an attempt to communicate those moments, they can never be shared.

All theories concerning the origins of emptiness are as good as useless, but once the process begins then the flame of life inside whoever embodies and inhabits that emptiness shall never be starved, but burn forever, paying for its permanence with the awareness of itself. Beauty still comes to this flame, scorching her wrists as she kneels to listen to the voice that chatters on to itself. Lisa heard enough of that too soon, and walked out.

When I go down to The Vault to drink, I search through chaos, looking for an angel to release. A drink for Merril! That is the reason for my evening at The Vault. Chaos can be disciplined, I suppose, by a chorus of something dependable — a chorus of England! Conducted from the heart. The heart of England, the heart of Merril.

The claret stings my dry lips. 'First of anything's always a bastard,' I say to myself. The Vault is a deserted underground cavern beneath the southern end of London Bridge, abandoned even by those whom death has not yet quite undone but left to sweat it out. It is a barn for an English harvest which has never been reaped.

Drinking down there in the dark, I begin to fissure chaos. On the cold table top I can see between my fingers a formation of concentric circles spreading out over England. I am their heart. Their heart is London, London is the heart of England, and I am the heart of London. Neither spreading oak of Tewkesbury nor serene church spire of Suffolk has a claim to the title of heart. A heart in the dark, Merril.

In the warmth of my claret I picture the surrounding golden shires. They are the plains of Heaven; above questioning, and above mortality. I have been feeling nervous all day, and now I can hear the chorus of the plains of Heaven. It comes down to me through the ceiling. Wilful in its nature, the glorious serenade falls down to my appreciative ears, scorning the traditional ascent into the pale and effeminate lychees of light that dangle from the skeletal lamp posts above.

It is a secular chorus. Searching for some faith away from the club, my national pride genuflects to the counterpoint of heavenly discord. The Church depresses me. The chorus works like an expectorant upon the clots of my depression, loosening attitude into anticipation. I feel that I have wanted secular truth, or money truth, and now I do not know what I want at all. For me, the candles are cold, or rather, they don't work anymore. Denying them, I need the light anyway, I cannot say how much. Truth goes into a darkening retrospect, and ecclesiastical relic. I see crimson light. There are black bubbles moving around in it, rising and falling in accordance with the nervous thermals of my mood. These bubbles mutilate my sense of vision, causing all proportions to blink. Needing light, but not candles, I order another bottle. Raising the freshly filled glass to my lips, I pause, watching my hand. 'Candles' bastard light,' I say to myself.

Outside it's crucifix carpark, the shadow of Southwark cathedral. A pavement level spasm of peach coloured light flexes the heart's muscle; a moist shift in the atmosphere derived from all that takes place in the night. Bloodied feathers settle onto drifts of coal dust as the frantic ramblings of the out of luck can be heard in shouts down weary rubber walkways that lead to empty platforms. I hate the epigrams of failure. Cogs worn smooth to the groove are best kicked out of the engine.

Jolting on a memory that flicks at my elbow, I hear the chorus convert into an eerie relay of prayer and response. I take a step backwards, spilling my drink. There follows a second of candlelit hesitation as my hands refuse to perform some token genuflection and then everything goes quiet again. I focus on the cigarette machine. It looks like a car. I get a mental image of the last Spitfire going over the Channel and I hear the engine splutter. 'No!' My shout echoes. Embarrassment.

A little later I feel a metallic, fruity saliva filling my mouth. I grind out my cigarette, trapping charcoal under my nails. I clamber upstairs and all the 'streetcries of old London' are the wrong way up. I get outside, squinting through the sweat that's got into my eyes and wander off. I am from Vauxhall to the Thames Barrier. I am a connecting space.

A drunken disgrace to my country, I can see a brutal portrait of myself as faithless patriot reflected in the river. I lean over the embankment and throw loose change into the water to try and break it up. The picture reforms monotonously. Over the water I can see the lights that shine on its surface. The light, the years, and the citizens — tiny pieces of white glass. They make a mosaic that spreads out all over London. All over England. I can see Individual Rights scattered across the pavement. They gleam softly under the lamps, phosphorescent fish lips gaping at the moon. Bad claret.

I walk on to Cleopatra's Needle, a folly that's been sunk to the bottom and refloated, a museum piece that's spent the best part of its life being sucked by silt. I greet it like an old friend.

At The Crypto-Amnesia Club I have given away most of my favourite things after drinking like this. There is not much left. So I sit on one of the raised public benches, as cold as iron, and take deep breaths. The city spins round like a ballroom globe, coercing a chaotic symmetry with the mosaic spread across it. London Bridge has fallen down. All the colours seem to begin and end in water, and each minute seems suspended in the silver guts of a chaos that I stand no hope of adjusting. I've never been the heart of anything, nor really had an angel to free, only Lisa, and she's nothing more than a shadow on the X-ray. But Lisa is my angel, and she is the depiction of a symptom within the diagnosis. She is neither life threatening, nor responsive to treatment.

In London I live on a vein of the sea. Bored or scared I watch the recreations from mud with an immense restlessness. There remains the possibility of continuing within this life sentence, all clauses subordinate and all meanings inevitable. An emptiness that spreads through me on the river past the limits of the city, and on to a constant widening of a sea arch. Each tide returns a handscrape of earth, some wet stones thrown back at my feet. From emptiness to emptiness, the mind and the body received. And Britannia, barnacled on her distant rock, has ocean debris in the kaleidoscope of her eyes. We mimic decay.

THREE

A Visit to the Museums

I am in the memory racket. This is a sideline to The Crypto-Amnesia Club as well as my professional enthusiasm. I take it personally. Like a star I have been hurled through the night of the world to come (via solipsism and drunkenness) to this — the big road, Kensington Gore. It's a fine afternoon for a memory man to take a trip to the museums and pay his humble tributes.

I have noticed around these parks that you never hear the Lost Boys complain. I am a Lost Boy, P. Pan a hero in my book. He was the one who had the sense to stay in Central London and not participate — not even age. He, Pan, is such a rare bird. He is scarce. He's my inspiration when I get drunk, he helps me to forget that I am the manager of the fashionable Crypto-Amnesia Club. Regarding my thoughts of Lisa he says, 'It's okay. It must be a great adventure, but times change . . .'

Going down from the parks to the golden shoeboxes of world knowledge I admire the way that they stand so handsome, rising up with the dignity of pyramids, places in which to loot and plunder from the looted and plundered — by time, or men, or both.

It makes me sad to see all these memories displayed under glass with only a dehumidifier for comfort. It makes me angry to see the exhibits spread out for the gawping public. Each of these objects is a memory, and there is no respect for their stories within these zoos. The museums force tricks of educational experience out of the old things spread out in them; with their letraset dynasties and primary coloured signposts. The sulking children and irritable couples wander about, pressing buttons and waiting for lights to flash. I prefer the dusty cabinets and illegible Latin tags — the arrogant obscurity developed by the half dead junior clerk. Ancient relics gasp out their memories like dead starlight under these conditions, and I should know, because I run a shrine to the process of forgetting, and I hear their gasps all the time.

Yet I can only understand memory alone. I have tried to slip this understanding under the side plate as it were, like a tip — I have tried to offer compassion, and let understanding ride in on compassion's coat tails. I have failed. I cannot forget my lover who catalysed my hatred of my job. It's a mess. I am trapped on all sides, and so I visit museums, trailing my coat and determined to join no side, either here with the anthropologists and gawpers, or back at the club with the idiot guests. Both this museum and The Crypto-Amnesia Club exhibit relics. Both attempt a cargo cult magic, trying to will a reality out of bits of the past and a load of bamboo models. A botched transubstantiation — we live in hope for a truth.

Lisa is only a model — she isn't real. She is real only in my memory, for that's where she is reconstituted, reanimated, filled in. I have yet to see Heaven walk on Earth at The Crypto-Amnesia Club, yet I am sure they have an artist's impression of Heaven . . . at the Geological Museum.

When I leave the museums I walk through Kensington Gardens with a nod to the lads, and then on to where Byron slumbers in front of the London Hilton: Byron stares at the Hilton, the Hilton dwarfs Byron. Poor Byron, on his traffic island, undermined by the pedestrian subway.

I follow the line of Green Park, a golden section, then turn north into Mayfair, a garbled route. There is a little garden in the heart of Mayfair, behind the US Services Chapel, South Audley Street, and here I stop, and draw deep breaths, and watch evening fall on the chestnut trees as a top-rent breeze comes like Mother to soothe the cares on my careworn face, the stress lines of memory.

An Imaginary Conversation.

'Hello my dear, how are you?'
'Oh. I feel sad this evening.'
'Sad? Why is that?'
'Everyone has forgotten about everyone else.'
'Oh well, it must be spring. Can you smell the hairspray?'
'Is the sun out? Is it evening already?'
'No my dear, it's you.'

My museum is a garden away from The Crypto-Amnesia Club.

FOUR

Who Loved These Gardens

I know nothing of life, or death. Here, in this garden, away from The Crypto-Amnesia Club, I consider how the sheer weight of embarrassment, self-reproach, self-disgust, and self-loathing might finally cause me to revolt against the course of my life. The truth of the matter is that this revolt only takes place in my mind. My mind revolts whilst I sit in a public garden. I am a city full of rebels. I can hear them smashing bottles on my streets. I am The Crypto-Amnesia Club, full of violent guests; I do nothing but house rebels, but neither my thoughts of revolt nor the rebels in my club are real — they are all fakes. There are no barricades here where I sit and watch the chestnut blossom, here in this public garden.

My guests and I are intrigued and inspired by the idea of change, yet we do nothing to carry out our plans. What with the anger and the hard, hot, dry-skinned sense of uselessness that we feel in the face of our immobility, we ought to do something. But my guests do not realise that they do nothing, and I scarcely remember what doing something is. Mostly there is vacancy, emptiness, Lisa, and disliking the guests who come to the club to impersonate forgetting. Despair sometimes makes my mind wander, and as the shadows lengthen my thoughts stray to the idea that I could be seen leaving a house around here, a flat package all wrapped up in brown paper under my arm. Clumsily carrying my parcel I would hail a taxi and drive away, hoping that no one had seen me. The parcel would contain a portrait of myself, or rather, an image of me. The portrait would be of a man hideously blemished, disfigured within a fraction of any likeness to myself, the sitter. It would be a map, the portrait of my revolt into immobility. A cross between a cartoon and an allegory: 'The Stowaway in Dry Dock.'

Each false start would be etched upon my features, each time I have said, 'Not yet...' a scar upon my face. The portrait I am imagining would be a portrait of someone who never got beyond self-obsession. To conclude — I would take the picture to Christie's Contemporary and ask for a valuation.

But this ridiculous imagining of amateur mysticism is just embarrassing; it takes place between the box of boutique tissues and the photograph of your best friend's bathroom, between the pack of shrink-wrapped tarot cards and the catalogue for the world as will and idea. I reject this stupid flight of fancy, and concentrate upon the shadows as they lengthen across the lawn, each centimetre bringing me closer to when I must hail a taxi, and go back to the office. I must convert my loneliness into strength, I must treat the problem of how much I miss Lisa as a comic opera. I must hang the whole sorry mess with a faulty set of fairy lights. With the aid of some strong drinks and a dedication to romanticising my past I shall overcome my loneliness by satisfying the demand for failure that exists within it; for as I (obviously) do not want to revolt against my life and therefore change it, I (obviously) must want to suffer in it.

If I am not content with my dim, blue, Venetian-blinded office, I can at least be happy in the knowledge that I am not joining in with the emotional fashion of The Crypto-Amnesia Club, that mental style common to my deluded, foolish guests and dubbed (by me) 'The Malvolio Syndrome'. The Malvolio Syndrome is an illness for people who have forgotten everything save their self-obsession. A rumour, or an image, or an attitude, wafts in at random through the smoked glass doors, and immediately the victims forget everything other than how best to identify with it. They tie the ribbons just so, wear the shirt buttoned, or unbuttoned, thus, and then they are all it — whatever it may be. It changes hourly, and then they can ring up all their friends to tell them about it, or go out and look at old versions in the museums. They excel at it. It scorches their wrists like a burn of Chinese whispers, but I reject it, preferring this garden that I have loved. Here where the flowers are undecided between early and late spring, I think of Lisa and The Crypto-Amnesia Club. The mazed rose, typically enough, knows not which is which, or what is what, and neither do I — other than that my love affair with Lisa should have worked, and let me out, and given me someone to sit here with.

The paths are white with blossom, the roads blue with evening. I cannot live properly without Lisa. I do not know where she is now. She never comes to the Club these days, but then who can blame her? (Why do I find excuses for her? She is not here now and I do not know where she is, or with whom. It's nothing, I know, and I'm sure that it will all be alright. All through spring I can tell the people I know that everything will be alright, that they aren't to worry, everything will be okay. 'It's okay,' I can say, holding them firmly by the elbow and leaning into their faces, 'It will be alright . . .' I wonder if I really would help someone by saying that? Someone who might otherwise have gone home and cried? Perhaps they would — because of my intervention — go home and be happy instead? I suppose not. Despair runs too cruel a Titanic, and the cabaret taking a trooper's attitude would seem extremely out of place.) But it may still all be alright. It may still all work out, and we will go shopping again, down South Audley Street, for luxury goods.

A false summer, a Malvolio summer, has possessed this garden I have loved. The breeze has softened, warming the air to pink. The leading on the chapel windows seems fine and precise, and the hyacinths are budding red, muscling the air with their scent, their petals inscribed with woe.

I think that Lisa will never return, or I can feel this in the early evening and glimpse it in the sunlight fading behind my back. I can do little or nothing to put a greater distance between myself and all the places that remind me of her. In my crypto-amnesia, all places are equidistant from an inner pearl of sadness, measured in memories.

It will rain tonight, bringing on summer, a sexy rain. It's time to go.

FIVE

Scrawling Wonderful Peter Pan

On the first of her seven pages, her week, Lisa could lay claim to little more than a scrawl. That was her all and everything as regards unique authorship.

Perhaps the scrawl had a meaning. Something legible to her eyes alone, or maybe it was all nothing more than a scrawl. I don't know, I wasn't there. A day's effort however, utterly and irrevocably spent feeling as though she were crawling on her hands and knees across an office floor. Crawling and dribbling against the unbearable light in a sixth floor window. Away from a vase of flowers perhaps, a spot of colour on a filing cabinet.

Of course, nobody would actually have seen her crawling, it wasn't what you'd call an activity, but that wouldn't matter. The scrawl would say that she was crawling and that was all that mattered.

Lisa ran all the way to Buckingham Palace, delivering notes for her boss. She arrived breathless, a heel broken somewhere along the dusty Mall. She sotod in the enormous car park, late afternoon, the sun setting. She didn't have to do anything.

'Here I am in the enormous car park,' she thought. 'Here I am . . .'

Her broken shoe made it painful to walk. She took off her shoes, her expensive court shoes. At least she didn't have dirty strips of elastoplast across the backs of her heels. At least she didn't look like somebody who bought cheap shoes that didn't fit. The road hurt her feet through her tights as she walked away.

Twilight brought a cloud of dust, blown all the way from the Serpentine basin to hang in the trees of Green Park, the golden section. The trees, in fullest leaf, looked white. The dusk turned the alkali dust on the foliage gold.

Lisa stood just inside the monumental railings at the south entrance to the park, her shoes in one hand, her scrawl in the other, a child discovering a larger field.

She would, she decided, stretch out beneath one of the trees. She would lie down right there in her expensive work clothes. She wouldn't move, it would be alright. She would watch the trees grow whiter as the park grew darker. She would listen to the slurred anthems of the traffic. There would be no need to draw curtains across her dozing deciduous world. She would weaken to find the scrawl gone away, the aching, all-fours, sick lurch of the useless day would be quite repressed. She would maintain her faith whilst nothing that she had ever done could ever (with the best, most compassionate will in the world) demonstrate anything to endorse it. This was when the trees were white, and life was largely a question of embarrassment, like leaving with your shoes under your arm, like negotiating the strange dusk of a failing affair.

Alone in the park, with no use for fantasy, her dresses strewn all over the floor at home and the powder warm on her cheeks, Lisa slept — despite the blanket of sharp sticks that were digging into her back, piercing her blouse, and breaking her skin as she shifted slightly.

Half awake for maybe ten seconds, Lisa thought that she could hear a boy's unbroken voice, although something was obviously wrong. There was drink in the air, and foul language; she thought she heard murderous screams. All these things, and all her subsequent fitfulness, did nothing save tunnel a deeper silence.

She knew, even as she slept, that she must go home. She had to go back to her flat in Chelsea. Her friends would surely be worried. Her rich friends. Gemma and Liz would have decided to ring up Marcus by now, to see if she was there. Knowing nothing of me they would decide that she was curled up on his sofa, her head lying in his blue wool lap. She wasn't.

Lisa remembered that it was her turn to take the rent around to the landlord. Each month, they took turns. Or so she seemed to remember. She couldn't be sure. Her ribs ached and ached from lying on the hard ground for so long. Maybe she had won a medal sometime, for bravery, for some little bit of human decency. For finding her way in the dark.

She stood up, bending down painfully to brush the dust off her black skirt with the back of her hand. She couldn't find her shoes anywhere.

Soon she would be home. She could say, 'You'll never guess what, I fell asleep in the park this evening — I hope you didn't worry.' Her rich friends would look at her with their regular brown eyes, inwardly diagnosing the nature of her problem without having the slightest knowledge of its symptoms. Their county good sense would lead them straight to some suitable explanation which they would then give to her. That was alright. Just as long as they didn't try to tamper with the truth. They would look upon the truth with strong disapproval anyway.

Lisa hated her rich friends' stares as she stood in the yellow light of the kitchen. She hated their concern. There was nothing to be concerned about. She had been tired. Her shoe had broken. She had lain down for a while in the park.

As the sky darkened into a blue rotunda and the second star to the right was high over Chelsea, Lisa knew that all the advice in the world would not dissuade her from her decision to leave Merril, London, and the UK.

SIX

The Beach

Oh yes well eventually you always end up there, at The Beach: a tarted up brasserie with stream-of-self-consciousness decor that strives towards bohemia but has somehow never made it. The acid-tongues out there call it The Desert, and maybe everyone calls it The Desert, just add people and stir for the heaviest ambience in town. They are always open. They never close. Half the crowd who take their sherry and seltzer at The Beach end up at the Crypto-Amnesia by midnight. Although the marbling-on-a-roll is looking a little tired these days, some kind of corporate identity has evolved that keeps a constant stream of youngsters in there, reciting lists to one another and going to the toilet in between sips of mutant aperitifs and filtered draughts of lukewarm gossip. There are tired flowers on the greasy zinc bar, and the air is filled with the stench of a thousand perfumes, every one of which produces an eye watering gas when confronted with its rivals. The house style is reputedly workman, heavy on the durable fabrics and designer haversacks; anything as long as it looks like you've been working. The crowd imagine the jobs that they could just have been doing, and because they are all assistants — mostly video film assistants — they compete strongly with one another to appear the most harassed and exhausted, which is difficult. They all affect to have sun-gun wrist, a swelling of the lower forearm due to steadying lighting rigs for too long between coffees.

The reason I broke a long respected rule and actually went to The Beach was to find Archer: a former habitué of the Crypto-Amnesia and now manager of The Beach. He has a drink problem.

He also sells art. You can tell this by his fringe and his nostrils, both of which are flared. He is an art pimp, and very anti-intellectual at that. He is in the anti-intellectual racket — a very safe place for a café patron and art-pimp to be. When I pushed my way through the wall of bespoke donkey jackets that surrounded the bar, I found Archer leaning against the Gaggia machine flipping through a new issue of 'Generating False Identities,' checking out the bad career moves and inwardly noting new sponsors. Archer is a self-styled stylist, a Frankenstein built by zombies to be a mortician. He claims to spend his nights off running time and motion studies in gay brothels, and his favourite joke is the one about the graphic designer and dry-mounting. His limit is sex.

He greeted me with an enthusiasm common to veteran bores, and then settled down to gossip. He had been to a party the night before. This made my blood run cold because he might have seen Lisa at it. (Lisa! The girl who forced me to witness the chilling transformation of friendship into politeness; the slow way down.) Archer says, 'It was really alright you know? There were all these people there at Chrissy knows who did that thing with Mingus Factory last year at the Grey Edge, and now they're doing a record because one of them knows this bloke who used to be Roxy Music's manager but now he does stuff with that guy with the hair, and he thought they were really outrageous and said . . .'

I wave him into silence. Archer's eyebrows hover like jump jets above the frames of his dark glasses, anticipating . . .

'Did you uhm, see Lisa there ah?'

'Lisa who? Oh! Lisa thingy right? No.'

Although my heart has been as chilled as oranges in cognac,

I somehow manage to forgive Archer everything he stands for and let him carry on telling his stories. I am safe now. So Archer flashes his bit of amateur mysticism around like a teenage fiancée her single solitaire and talks of the legends currently being made. They are all alike.

Archer seems to say: 'But I am beautiful; and I have brains too; and my beauty is troubled by my brains. I cannot stand the strain of the best of all possible worlds . . .'

I don't believe him. He is just what you would expect of someone who spent the brief springtime of his life all cooped up in The Crypto-Amnesia Club, down there in the dark, making phone calls.

Archer has a parting shot; a fleshwound inflicted with the exquisite taste of someone who assumes that pain is pleasurable. He says, 'Oh, I'm having this dinner party soon right? And I've asked Lisa to it . . . You must come — and bring a little friend — I'm sure you've got hundreds . . .'

I wander off to the toilets. On the powder grey wall above the marblesque 'Continentale' hand basin, a tertiary educated debate has been commenced in various widths of mapping pen, the subject of which is the derivative ironies of the design style of The Beach. Beneath the last entry — a clever reference to Paolozzi incorporating three Italianate puns — some misfit has scrawled with the blade of a screwdriver: CUNT.

SEVEN

Orpheus Ignored: Part One

Archer's invitation to his dinner party acted as an amphetamine upon me, bringing, as it did, a sense of urgency and speed to my days. The possibility of seeing Lisa again was accompanied by the obvious notion that once reunited we would obviously start our affair all over again.

Seized with this speed, I went for long walks around the City of London, right away from the City of Westminister, and deep into the square mile. Through the wards and wardrobes, the courtyards and the building sites I followed a random passage daily. The shrapnel wounds in the corporate masonry would jerk my eyes towards the towering acres of smoked glass, there to stare at the trails of steam curling out from the air vents and the dribbles of shredded paper that spewed from the grilled mouths of waste disposal chutes.

The City is a strange land, and I have often thought of taking out a lease somewhere in it to open a new club. Research late into the winter nights had taught me that few people are out on the streets after the offices throw out their workforce, and those who remain in the empty playground seem to be quite happy with their eighteenth century snug and a pint or two of ale. My plan, therefore, to open a nightclub called The Killer Moth, would seem less than likely to succeed. So now I use the City as a park, day out, full of surprises, and a place where I have no influence or justification.

It is the enormity of the square mile that intrigues me; the fact that it must be at least seven miles across, and yet there is always room for a new development, some elbow room for the sunset. On the bronzed perimeters, at daybreak, with the sun beginning to warm the cement mixers, you can stand and see the latest sites. The places where only the very new survives. The vast and untenanted, the thought of in Chicago, the financed in the Gulf, the designed in Italy, and the owned by the anonymous Lion. Intermediate Technology Systems Consultancy will soon be here. Neighbour to Finance Investment Services (Vaduz). To have that power, the power of obscurity at a dizzy height, the high on the lonely horizon — to not even know what industries one is captain of anymore; to cease caring altogether about the visible and simply play with new sculptures that plate-tectonically reunite the constantly shifting values of abstract currencies — maybe that's a life. These meanderings in the shadow of the Mansion House did nothing whatsover to calm my sense of urgency. I did not receive the merciful tranquility of an afternoon on the riverbank, over the worst and getting things straight.

One day I returned home through the West End; up near Marble Arch on the edge of Little Saudi, and then pursuing the old steakhouse route towards Mayfair. My speed was almost too much to bear. I was walking with a new direction; walking towards the time I would be going to Archer's dinner party, there, perhaps, to see Lisa, and herein lay my hope and my speed, my glimpse of red on the window pane. Lunchtime crowds in harmless blue raincoats parted to let me pass. The sporeclouds of the west-end work force blew all around me. I kicked out playfully at stacks of rubbish outside wine bars, I bought myself things.

And then, suddenly, with no warning, I dropped; not slowed down, or broken, but simply caved in on my mood. Like a helium balloon suddenly ripped with a velcro tear. Why had I bought these flowers? Why this bottle of Rémy Martin? Why had I believed, if only for a moment, in a spring that would reneweth all understanding? I walked on slowly to Green Park station, unable to think of walking any further, for walking is an exhausting conversation, and I had not got the strength. It is frightening when the illusion of direction can inspire such speed without fuel. Maybe I was not ready to leave The Crypto-Amnesia Club, maybe I was only good for a gentle wheeling around.

In the station I saw the locust men from surrounding corporations all blurring into one raincoat and one soft scarf. They had a direction. I assume. They looked like the admin team for the Last Symposium, sharpening their prejudices on the station furniture, ready to cast their collective suspicions upon the likelihood of my ever seeing Lisa again.

'Merril!' they seemed to shout, 'You are wrong. Not only are you mad, you are pitifully equipped to deal with it.' And so on, down the tunnel that takes me home beneath the silver streets of this, the greatest of all cities in this Land of Hope and Glory.

Given time maybe I could be happy with these stupid moods. Perhaps I want them. I seem to have spent half my life in and out of institutions like these moods; the white unfurnished rooms of the non-drip glossy, where Lisa reaches her gloved hand out to me, her black-gloved, musk-scented hand. Her features balance with the finger that she stretches out to touch my finger (my naked, scratched finger), and then it is Eve creating Adam, just another cry for help. This is totally unlike the Adam creating Adam moods that fill to brimming the eighty minutes of an Eastcheap Happy Hour, Beastlies perhaps, with the soup in a basket and the dark green chairs, men falling into blackboard menus, their eyes like silicon chips in a state of rum and black.

Travelling on the underground I realize that Lisa has become two quite separate emotional states; she is both a missed person and a missing person; this double identity recasting her in my life as a faraway war; a crisis perceived as merely theoretical when one can distance oneself from the curfew and the food queue. Her being missed and her being missing are now merging into one thing, and that thing is relevant to me inasmuch as it becomes the object of a rescue, a mercy dash, a white charge. I am mesmerised by this neon in the Stygian darkness, this thing, and I simply go for it, heroic and replaceable, but wanting of a plan.

EIGHT

Orpheus Ignored: Part Two

There is so much to this affair, which is simply a glass of water coloured with memory. I wonder (as I travel ridiculous and stationary up the escalator at the other end) whether Lisa ever considered love as an appreciation of another person's history? That is, to adore the lingering implications of your lover's growing up? To be in love with a nostalgia for somebody; to be in love in order to witness the latest stages of your lover's evolution. I don't know. My hat tilts on the back of my head, my trouser turn-ups are soaked, my glasses slide down to perch on the end of my nose. Cigarette. I feel tired.

Now that the speed has died down, I can clearly remember a visit that I paid to a girl who I hardly knew, on the eve of her wedding. She had asked me round because we hardly knew each other, and she didn't want to be distracted by intimacy on that eve. She wanted to mime a sentimental evening and still get an early night. She was sitting in the room where she had spent most of her life, preparing to quit it once over by her commitment to a change the following day. She would return to the room from time to time, but under different circumstances.

She was complete in that room, surrounded by her souvenirs and her relics, the epiphenomena of a life: the fluffy toys won for her by some former boyfriend at a coastal fair years ago, the strata of cosmetics (above the washstand) that dated back to the original Body Shop and then, finally, the bottom line — the row of twenty pairs of shoes, spread out like a crescendo on a creased sheet of music. The spoils of a thousand shopping trips, the evidence of a thousand rainy afternoons in bad-tempered shops. From the plimsolls rebelliously worn to school, to the court shoes worn once to a friend's wedding, to the scuffed and despised work shoes, to the final sad lustre of the catalogue bridal slippers — white shells in a rockpool of tissue paper. Her fiancé was marrying a collection of shoes, scorched by hot pavements and frozen by bus stop sleet.

And so I reached home. I rarely see my home, being so much at the club. My rooms are spacious, top floor, random. The rooms are mostly empty, and they have rough edges. Everything in them seems to float slightly: the fabrics, the wires and the paintwork. As I sat there late into the spring night, I could see the treetops parallel to the open window beginning to bud, and a ripple of green was lapping the sill. I sat in the biggest room, trying to concentrate on thinking, and my thoughts returned to Lisa, Archer and the mission. As yet I have received no change of address card from Lisa, postmarked Traitors' Gate, or post-marked Marie Céleste. Nothing. So I sat there by the open window in the dark, sprawled in an anonymous blue suit, my tie loosened and my collar unbuttoned. I looked at myself in the mirror and pondered on what the erosion of myself by memory has left behind to live in the suit. It has left a sea arch for the fluid of states of mind to flow through, again and again. On this stream all things pass by, but bring with them no real nutrition, just spiritual anorexia, the soul rejecting the input of emotions, emotion being the acid in my mind's stomach. So I sat there in the cool night air, curing nausea with a breeze, if only for a while, and waiting for daybreak. The comfort of the revealed rooftops at dawn, the chorus of birdsong.

Once there was a voice in me, and now we all seem to speak in tongues, each voicing variations of itself, carving out an identity-delta, a mouth at the edge of the sea, battered by impassable currents. No more songs of innocence at The Crypto-Amnesia Club. I ought to have married Lisa and not allowed myself to get into this mess. Out in the square I can hear two drunk girls. They seem to be screaming spiteful rumours up to my window. Their abuse slides in on the spring air with a sickly scent of oranges. These two furies twist once in a swirl of taffeta and are gone, leaving me full of dark imaginings, jerked into a nervous sleep.

Waking at noon, the windows full of blue sky. This sunny morning, its thin air thickening to warmth on the pavements, the day has been made for happy couples to stroll through. When evening comes, I shall look out over London and see the golden white buildings as the roar falls away over Knightsbridge, a cloud of perfume and petrol hanging in the air behind it. In the London evening, in all the cooling bars, short barmen will be polishing glasses, happy among the virginal coleslaws. The little wooden tables, smelling of sackcloth and hairspray, will await new drinkers. The streets will clear with a noise like the felling of a giant redwood tree as a hundred thousand bags of shopping will be thrown down on a hundred thousand sofas and the shoppers run their baths. All will be well in the lovers' world where a bunch of flame cerise freesias are spread across the skyline.

And when this evening comes, as the poor are sweating around Eros, the rich will be sitting in Jermyn Street bars, there to place with stubby finger ends the delicate glasses of electrochilled Nierstein on the edges of wickerwork tables.

With an anticipatory frisson, the theatre audiences of London will squeak excitably on their black plastic barstools, waiting to be entertained. 'Hello,' they say, 'Hello Janet, hello — I've been waiting for hours round the corner . . .'

Young professionals in their casual clothes will sprawl in

their fatty opulence throughout the greater suburbs, bullying their pretty young wives, and mending things in a temper.

It will all be like this as I taxi to the club. I shall drift by the Mayfair restaurants, envying them their wide striped awnings and little tubs of pavement conifers. But each minute — although nobody could care less — will be bringing me closer to Archer's dinner party, and the chance to see Lisa. For this occasion I must learn some magic, a trick of speech or a sleight of hand and for this sorcery I must have an apprentice. Before I go out tonight I shall telephone Amelia, my old friend, and ask her to help. Amelia will help me at Archer's dinner party, if she's not busy.

NINE

Yellow House With Young People

I first met Amelia some years ago. She was leaning against the wall outside a party, her arms folded, staring at the pavement. It had been a terrible party, not least for Amelia, who considered it a turning point in her life.

Damp primroses had stroked the ankles of the girls as they made their way up an unfamiliar path to the yellow house. There was lightning overhead, but no rain.

And there, always around (waiting in front of shops, loitering moodily beside the car, standing in the red garden), were the boyfriends. The puppy-fat pretty, the six-feet-two, the ever-so-slightly psychotic and jealous. Born to be boyfriends and little else.

The yellow house in the provincial city stood tall and old in its residential suburb. A ziggurat built by some successful northern merchant, it spiralled up in layers of grey windows, trailing virginia creeper through the cobwebbed corners of their frames. Heavy velvet curtains kept the light out.

In the garden, the unpleasant, predatory smell of patchouli was desecrating the spring evening. Beneath the darkening porch a knot of young people held the party together. A boyfriend was talking with the grim determination of a mist bewitched gattling gun into a semi-circle of polite young people, all of whom wore black. The boyfriend looked both aimless and ruthless.

Soon, music came wafting through the old house, curling its over-familiar fingers around the wooden bannisters, stirring people's drinks with its fingernails. The music took the girlfriends back to the semi-precious lustre of their teenage weekends, its saucy beat bringing a sparkle to the rhinestone tiaras of the virgin brides. The air smelt sweet and green, and a boyfriend commanded attention from his attractive girlfriend, Amelia, dressed in black, apparent by her silence, and older than her partner.

Amelia had learnt the penalty for personality in the rich summer evening traumas of her early adolescence; the flinging of herself on the childhood quilt, dressed to go out but determined in the last five minutes not to.

She had endured the hurt and reproachful sulks of her boyfriends time after time. She had taken all the sullen and sentimental criticism that sheet swaddled, small-hours baby-talk can throw up. Her role at the party was maternal. She played at being a mother substitute for the sake of some peace and quiet. Her boyfriend was happy; he always wanted to smack his mother. Amelia flattered and encouraged him. When they went to parties she dressed him.

'Oh you look nice in that . . .'

Appeased, he would allow her to mascara his eyes. It would lend to his rigorous masculinity the veneer of liberalism and non-conformity that he must appropriate if he was to remain head and shoulders above the crowd and sure of his bedtime delights.

Out in the road, swollen raindrops were beginning to smash all over the roofs of the cars. On the staircase, neglected or deserted girlfriends were sitting with their sympathetic best friends. The best friends were trying to prove a personal, independent point. Sitting on the stairs was for them a tactical manoeuvre in a long-term strategic fight against indifference. Looking over the tops of their drinks, the girls on the staircase pretended to talk. The best friends were well turned out. They blew their blowdried fringes out of their eyes and felt humid beneath their blusher.

Amelia talked. Whilst she was talking she recalled the stretch of artificially turfed recreational ground outside her hall of residence. The ground was soaking wet beneath the glow of a line of lonely lamp posts, erected by someone with a builder's plan who knew more than Amelia about what they should be lighting. That person maybe also knew about the empty room between Amelia's and the girl down the corridor's. When the mist rolls over Bradford again there will still be the empty room between the two with clock radios. This empty room is like a place on the edge of a desert. Amelia had all this in the foreground of her mind. The taste of mud and nail polish remover was in her drink. She could feel looseleaf paper between her fingers. She could hear the sound of a radio as if it were muted by several thin walls. In the empty room in the foreground of her mind she was rolling semi-dressed across her bed, dragging the covers down onto the floor and clasping herself in the uncurtained darkness. She was alone, the rooms on either side, inhabited or not inhabited. In the background of her mind was confusion. It seeped through into her mental picture of a room with no curtains.

In the yellow house the ground floor rooms had been cleared of furniture. The pictures had been taken off the walls. Over the mantelpiece there remained a large mirror in a black frame. In front of it, Amelia's boyfriend was talking about photography. Amelia looked away. She would not be Thisbe to his Pentax. There were so many of these boyfriends she thought, all quite interchangeable it seemed. Deep were their desires, and deeper still the gratification that many of them found therein.

The thunder rolled away to the green hills on the far side of the motorway.

'Tell me that you're miserable.' That is what Amelia wanted to say that night to her boyfriend. She didn't. Instead she gave him a look that was generous in its meaning. The shine in her eyes was not from tears. It was savage pointillism. There was gin, and ice, and moonlight in her eyes. There was anger there too. There was, 'Get out of my life. I hate you,' and there was, 'Why did you say that? Do you enjoy hurting me?'

Amelia's muscles tightened beneath her black shirt. Her jet necklace suddenly felt sharp. There was, 'Do you remember the way I walked towards you from the car when we stopped by a village that winter afternoon?'

Her boyfriend's eyes softened. His brown, waterlogged eyes, in which the significance of her looks contracted root-rot. His eyes were searching for new beginnings under an August sky, over-fertile in their determination. His eyes said, 'Now . . .' and his eyes said, 'Hey . . .' There was fear, hatred and curiosity flowing between their eyes. Her hard eyes were carbon under extreme pressure, coal and diamonds, the tear ducts pricking. The pre-history inside Amelia pushed the present into a wall to keep him out. It no longer had anything to do with him, that thing, their moment. She went outside to lean against a wall. He followed her.

She said, 'I can't see you anymore.' A moment earlier, the thought had seemed unthinkable. Now, beneath the dripping lime trees, so green above her black, the thought was perfectly straightforward. 'I cannot . . .'

And then fashion, the ultimate fiction — how blatantly it celebrated the insincerity of its narrative. Her scarf had not suggested, her black skirt had not prophesied, her black shirt had not . . .

Beneath the fabrics, Amelia's body, in assumed repose, invisible. Her drop earrings had not warned, her shadowed eyes, dyed eyelashes, powdered cheeks, heightened cheek-bones, glossed lips, perfumed neck, varnished nails, pencilled eyebrows . . . none of these had hinted that her story would have this twist. The theme had been so beautifully obscured by all these lovely adjectives.

'I will not see you anymore . . .' And now, into the distant past, the secret landscape of their beginning. There had, of course, once been a secret room for them. Potent with enchantment it had looked out onto a sunny garden where their English summer burned the grass and dried the appletrees. That room too, had been emptied of furniture. Her heels had echoed across the bare floorboards that hot afternoon, and after she had locked the door his heart had beaten faster at the sight of her back.

In front of the yellow house this was being mocked. The memories of hand reaching to hand and mouth reaching to mouth were all mildewing to green in the cold damp of that suddenly broken into room.

You could have called Amelia's face a mask that night. He maybe did out of revenge. But it was a face, not a mask, and warm to the touch and pleasing to the eye. The boyfriend lost her that night at the yellow house, so gone, and gone for good, for ever and ever, before death could them part.

That was how I first met Amelia. She's changed a lot since then.

TEN

Amelia and the Fruit Salad

All these years later Amelia is a new person. One day she will be a big star I expect. She has the only good copy of the pair of red shoes that Dorothy wore in Oz. She glitters scarlet up the dark staircase to my rooms. She works in a shop now. Her hair is black and shining. Amelia has blue eyes that also shine. They shine, 'Do you really believe in The Crypto-Amnesia Club? I mean now . . .'

On the subject of Lisa, Amelia says, 'Well is that wicked old witch really dead? I mean now . . .' But Amelia is an old friend, and she will not take it in the wrong way when I say, 'Amelia . . . Amelia, will you come with me to Archer's dinner party? I'm scared to go alone.'

'Hmmm,' said Amelia, 'Hmmm. Yes. I will. If, on one condition, if we can make a fruit salad together to take with us.'

'You drive a hard bargain Amelia,' I replied, 'but okay, it's a deal.' And so without a second thought for the work involved I rang the fruitshop and ordered lots of fruit, secular and exotic.

These days food is tremendously important, and Amelia understands that. Amelia had worked out (quite rightly) that one thing we would have to do if we were going to go to the dinner party was take some food with us. Something of our very own; something that was what we wanted to say. Amelia and I looked at the big box of fruit in the middle of my floor, and began to design our fruit salad. The colours lent themselves to the richly pre-Raphael: medieval reds and blues, freshened with yellow, white, and black; the whole image fixed and varnished with fruit juice and liqueur.

'Well,' we said, 'well . . .'

Amelia was fresh with the afternoon breeze, leaning out of my window to enjoy the fine spring weather. She seemed to be black and white and red.

We strayed into the kitchen and sharpened our knives, both considering the fruit for the slaughter. Amelia happily began to dissect a pineapple.

I watched Amelia absorbed in her work. So she really did work in a shop. Resting her weight on one leg, she stood elegantly before the table and, rolling up the sleeves of her crisp white shirt, hacked away at the pineapple with her knife until a stream of juice ran down her arm. She sucked the juice away, her lipstick leaving scarlet bruises on her arm.

I remembered how Lisa used to suck the blood out of paper cuts. This was part of the legacy of phoney erotica that she'd gone and left me with. How lamely the mind tries to compensate for sexual loss with its own perverse gymnastics. We pay for intimacy with self-confidence.

I poured boiling water on to the blade of my flick knife, the one that Lisa had bought for me in Milan station. When the blade was clean and burning I got to work on the peaches.

So all through the spring afternoon we peeled and carved and cut and chopped; with white and red grapes, and apples and lychees, and bananas and mangoes and guava and tangerines and kiwi fruit and . . . We did not notice the light begin to fade across the square, the trees gradually darken outside the window.

With lemon juice we made a base for the salad, Amelia's natural sense of occasion inspiring her to top the whole thing up with half a pint of framboise. The medieval colours and suprematist shapes stood glistening in the cut glass bowl like an offering. Frowning with concentration, Amelia tried a spoonful. Resting her hand on the table top, poised like a priestess awaiting a call, she tentatively raised the silver spoon to her lips. By the light of a dozen candles, Amelia whispered, 'Success!'

Our creation safely stored in the fridge, we paused to consider nightfall, my night off, peace.

It occured to me, as I stood in the vague blue room with Amelia, that a solution to my anxiety could lie in the notion of simply never moving again. Never go anywhere. Movement had been Lisa's big mistake, she moved with a bodily gentleness into a portfolio of violent people. She got caught up with the hectic and the obscene, and now she is lost forever on distant streets and different sheets, when she was meant for better or worse to be mine. I ought to be reasonable about this, but there is little reason in it.

Even Amelia, so far from the yellow house and all it stood for, is still running. That is why she came here today. Looking for a staircase to clatter up, away from the party she is supposed to be attending with her latest boyfriend. I missed my teenage life. Lisa told me, however, of startled girls in home counties gardens on humid July nights, clammy lace against limp rhododendrons and unformed imaginations seizing up for life in the wake of frustrated desires.

Archer's dinner party was the following evening, and all I wanted was to walk by the river instead. All the connections in my plan were faulty, a charred fusebox hanging off the wall between the medium and the message. I wanted to lie in Amelia's arms, her graceful wonderful, toughboy arms, and think about nothing at all. I am sometimes capable of thinking of nothing, but generally my head is full of some mangled television or other.

In the face of beauty we are either silent or articulate. I looked at Amelia and had nothing to say. Feeling drowsy she had slipped off her shoes and was sprawled in an armchair. One of the shoes had fallen against the other, sparkling red in the darkness beneath the chair, Christmas wrapping under evergreen lights. With the canvas blinds pulled down and London beyond, we fell asleep in separate chairs.

Amelia and I woke up from our separate dreams of flight. It was a southern morning, a glimpse of Italy until you really looked. My dreams had been interspersed with adverts for priceless products. We will spend the rest of our lives getting ready for dinner, Amelia and I. Several moths will hit several lamps before they rewire my forsaken bridal church with cold neon.

Waking with Amelia in the rare morning, I thought of all the expensive people who would be coming to Archer's party that evening. They would all be the same; in midnight blue and trailing jewellery they would surround their host, hinting generously, if only for an evening, that not one of them would be so offensive as to treat him like the poor drunkard he is. I do not know whether honesty would be kinder under these circumstances. The guests would represent themselves in the strip of light above their frosted personalised number plates, and in the milky triangles of light that scattered from their jewels.

Most of my life was in the gifts that I gave to Lisa and which she holds even now in her relaxed fist — or do I flatter myself? I gave her earrings, bracelets, silk scarves and necklaces. Breaking rocks in the hot sun, I fought the law and Lisa won. All that ice will never melt as long as it is in her care. I think she perhaps loved me only in a rare moment of weakness, but tonight, should we meet, I hope that she will remember the flowers in the vase, the sunlight on the wall, and the battered deckchairs on the beach of our dreams now that it's always October. Will I have to be bland to be credible tonight, Lisa? I won't dance, so don't ask me — don't even try. She is Ungaro's Bird of Paradise, Lisa, with her lipstick and her veil, and she will smile on seeing our fruit salad. It is for the Eve in her; one apple was never enough for Lisa so she must look upon the fruit salad as a back payment.

Amelia was sitting on the window sill, sipping tea. She was thinking about her boyfriend, whom she tries so hard to like. She is trying to decide whether to tell him that she is going out with me this evening. She can picture the scene already, her scarlet nails drumming on the dialling buttons, the ticker-ticker rhythm of the lines connecting, her blue eyes lowered. And then:

'Hello . . .'

'Oh hi. Where are you?'

'Merril's,' (and she blacks in the eyes on the cover of 'Vogue').

'Oh. . .'

'. . .'

'I'm going out for dinner. I'm making up the numbers . . .'

'Oh. Uh.'

It will be the story of Oh. Amelia doesn't really like her boyfriend anymore. She did once, and then she sort-of did, and now she doesn't. She feels like that about it, wearied by the thought of getting out but so indifferent that she can have a good time none the less. I feel rather sorry for her boyfriend. But then.

Sitting on the window sill, one leg drawn up, her chin resting on her knee, Amelia looks like the young Louise Brooks. It would be nice to go out for dinner with her if only the situation was different. I want to make it different, but feel powerless. If I see Lisa, perhaps things will be different, but this is not necessarily true. Only Lisa knows just how high up the beach the next wave will break.

ELEVEN

10,000 Green Bottles

Archer's alcoholism was little different from anybody else's: a secret life that had become too cumbersome, too conspicuous to pass undetected any longer by those who knew him at all well. His drinking caused the decay out of which the strange flowers of his colourful personality grew.

His illness had really set in during the unusually hot months of the previous summer — just before I had started seeing Lisa — and throughout that time I heard of little else save the catalogue of crises that befell him when drunk. He was continually drunk, living in a constant state of night-marish nausea between the heat and the drink. He claimed that the weather made him thirsty.

That summer there was no breath of fresh air — not the slightest breeze. If you lit a cigarette in the street the smoke just stayed where it was as you walked away from it, shorter of breath and drier of mouth, all liquid refreshment futile.

The sky was a constant luminous white. Around where the sun maybe was, there were a few dirty smudges. The sky was like a bruised face. There was no drop in the temperature come nightfall, or only a few degrees. In the airless night the sheets on lovers' beds were like sticky beer mats. The lovers would lie there, side by side and wide awake, the duvet that heals all crisis thrown onto the floor, the nakedness used to ritualised desire now evidence of corporeal frailty.

The West End stank. Invisible strata of rotten-sweet air blew out from extractor fans, and squadrons of flies pecked in and out of badly sealed garbage bags. A big car crawled up the Westway at fifteen miles an hour; elsewhere a staircase took all evening to darken.

There was nothing left to describe save lethargy; nothing in the whole of London except that Archer, sticking to his shirt, had just seen the best years of his life served up to him on a drooping palm leaf with a twist of lemon on the side. He drank more whisky, and then sat around and looked at them. He knew that they were the best years of his life because they had cost him so much.

'So this,' he said to himself, 'this thing . . .'

Another evening he fell over and cut his head on the pavement in Holborn. He wondered why he couldn't see. Everything was soft, and dark. With a gentle, puzzled look, Archer studied the stickiness on his finger ends and cheerfully congratulated himself on making the connection with his falling over.

'Plenty more where that came from,' he boomed.

Pressing a handkerchief to his forehead with one hand whilst trying to unscrew the top off a half bottle of Bells in his pocket with the other, he promptly tripped over the curb and fell directly into the path of a despatch rider, racing home to see his girlfriend. It seemed to Archer as though the rider had opened his arms, as if in welcome, at the very last moment. And then . . .

The rider was lying on the other side of the street with multiple fractures, bleeding heavily; Archer had lain down in the road and studied the reversed neon signature of a chemist's sign in the jack-knifed mirror of the crumpled bike. It was brilliant blue above the rooftops of Holborn, and in the hot silence of the street you could hear a pin drop.

By early September, the drink was beginning to make Archer violent, and this became apparent during a dinner date that, when sober, he had been looking forward to tremendously.

The evening had been going well, but then, at one in the morning, Archer had suddenly realised with a growing sense of outrage that his wit was turning into mere bombast, his date no longer laughing.

Feeling increasingly hot, Archer had tried to joke with her as they made their way through Berkeley Square, confusedly believing that this would lead him to her bed. She wasn't even listening. Leaning over the curb she was nervously trying to flag a taxi. They all had their hire lights off. The drivers shrugged at her as they passed.

Archer blinked in the night air. 'See here!' he shouted pompously, 'What have I done wrong all of a sudden? I thought we were supposed to be having a nice time?' She made an irritated, clicking noise with her tongue. 'It's late,' she said, 'I'm really tired. I had a busy day.' Without pausing for thought Archer bloodied her eye with the back of his hand.

As she gasped little screams and began to run, he brought up the contents of his stomach. Two hundred metres down the street Archer's escort was surrounded by a group of people, some of whom were trying to make him out in the darkness. Clutching his stomach and panting for breath, Archer sat down heavily in a doorway; a wet sack dumped on a mudbank.

The weather finally broke with a massive thunderstorm. People walked around more quickly again. Shopgirls laughed as they dressed a dummy, pins in the corners of their mouths — a novelty to be in a big pavement window looking out at the morning crowds in Oxford Street.

In the big offices, at mid morning, people up and down the strange hierarchies stirred scum lines of powdered milk into mugs of instant coffee. The mugs had stupid slogans printed on them: 'I Don't Like Monday Morning,' or 'Coffee Drinkers Make Better Lovers,' or 'In Case of Emergency, Buy Me A Drink.'

Archer looked around in the cooler air on his way to The Beach and realised he had survived something — temporarily. He saw the great caravan of the fairly interesting and the moderately impressive sweeping through the streets of London and still saw himself as a straggler, hiding in his bar, trying to reconcile romantic intoxication with wanton inebriation — it was for this reason that he continued giving his flamboyant dinner parties.

TWELVE

With Archer at Short Hemline

Archer was waiting to receive his guests by the bar at Short Hemline, a brand new restaurant which he had chosen as the venue for his party. Amelia and I were among the first to arrive, sweeping through the swing doors and passing our clingfilmed fruit salad into the respectful and unquestioning care of the head waiter. Archer was impressed by the fruit salad because he loved people to be creative.

'That's so like you,' he beamed, pleased to have a talking point, 'and how is the night club business?'

'Dark mostly,' I replied, unable to think of anything whatsoever to say. 'Dark mostly.'

'Well get a drink and forget all about your troubles; but Who . . .' (he gestured to Amelia, radiant in her scarlet fur coat) '. . . is This?'

'Amelia, Archer; Archer, Amelia.'

'How nice to meet you at last.'

'Uh huh. Hello Archer.'

We were waved down a line of waiters, the last of whom took us to a broad, low ceilinged alcove where a table for twelve was laid. The walls of the alcove were an eggshell blue, flecked with traces of brilliant orange.

All things are arbitrary in this service industry world except for the lustre with which Short Hemline shines, rich, and minimal, and fresh. The days of the night club are surely numbered. The clubs will die. People go out for dinner instead, and outside the property agents' boards flutter like seagulls. Intravenous apathy from a plastic bag of gin and lemonade, a drip dangling high over London from the top of the new Lloyds building. What has happened to London? It's like trying to kick start a tube of hair gel. 'Tennax,' Latin maybe, meaning 'hair gel.' Nobody has anything much to say to anyone else.

I roamed round the table, checking the place names. Lisa is not even coming. No place marked 'Lisa' at this table. I told Amelia, 'Uh . . . Lisa isn't coming.'

Amelia smiled, adjusting an earring. 'Well it'll be alright,' she said, 'everything will be alright. Just enjoy the food.' And Amelia turned to talk to her neighbour, a reticent red-head who thought she knew someone who worked in the shop where Amelia had bought her coat.

Spring had anticipated my boredom and invented nouvelle cuisine. All by itself perhaps, with a flurry of crocuses and a soft refreshing rain. This four-hour, five-course dinner would become a long conversation with an abstract painting. We were, after all, the Kiwi Fruit Generation. Undoubtedly the fleshy green hemispheres of fruit arranged on white china to the counterpoint of a rhomboid of strawberry has to mean something. But what of perseverance? I could lay claim to having endured The Crypto-Amnesia Club, and Lisa, but beyond that there was a vague something that I still felt myself to be designing. The Short Hemline was a good place to sit and consider that design. Its next move was still struggling in a net of tissue and research, everyone was kind of standing around not saying anything while they waited for it to appear. Perhaps they were all saving up to buy one just like it — whatever it turned out to be.

I looked at the exquisite table bouquets, strangely overcome with immense nostalgia for the dim blue office of The Crypto-Amnesia Club. I had only been away from it a day and a half. I remembered the bunches of freesias that were delivered to me daily, their scent, all mingled with fresh water and cellophane, bursting into the office. I think that Amelia understood these things. I don't believe Lisa did. I wish I loved Amelia. I am thirty-three and sitting in the Short Hemline with nothing in my mind except a single cipher code-named 'Lisa.' I am sick of the sound of the word. The rest is art history.

It seems that when we part from somebody, or when a divorce happens, we refer to the departed lover as though they were dead:

'What was she like?'

'Oh, she was . . .'

or,

'My girlfriend was a real angel.'

'Yes, but did she fly?'

We kill off those we abandon, or those who abandon us. I suppose it is convenient. It tames the pain, it distances the enemy, or makes the enemy acceptable — it obscures emotion. I join hands with those for whom everything is simply implied, like the food — architectural mousses, hinged with endive, the mousse in question, being offal based, benefiting no end from its presentation.

As course followed course in the emotional liquidiser of Archer's party, I began to consider the Short Hemline as a temple. I thought about reading prophecies from the calligraphy of shapes and sauces that were arranged like Delphic guts on the octagonal white plates. I was eating all the prophecies, distinguishing the trace of fennel in the mist of chives, appreciating the mango à la menthe with the tiny breast of partridge, circumflexed with an emblematic dash of red pepper.

The pale blue walls with their hint of anxiety were disturbed only by huge mirrors, plain and unembossed, designed for looking into, not at. The light fittings all suggested an English surrealism; cast iron bouquets of garden flowers, enamelled to pale and powdery colours, the whole construction appearing to float from the powder blue ceiling.

'Lord have mercy upon us and deliver us from surrealism.' That must have been Archer's prayer. Surrealism was the foundation of Short Hemline, however delicate. The spotless white linen of the table cloths, the brilliance of the glasses — all the simple elegance of the place was aimed at leaving the diner's sense open for full enjoyment of the food. There was no distraction within the themeless interior, and likewise no certainty. I cannot explain this sense of unease. Nothing was itself, just voices. 'Down will come Babel, baby and all . . .' I cannot understand the guests. They were all called things like Bronchitis. They knew that raspberry vinegar was good for marinating lamb, and that lamb should be cooked on hay. They were bathroom experts.

I did not speak to anyone much. I told a few people that everything was going to be alright. I sought Amelia's hand beneath the table but couldn't find it. I admired the clever vanilla motif on the chocolate parfait. I thought about a vampire panicking at Cranks. Every so often Archer stared at me through half shut eyes and then smiled unpleasantly to himself. I pitied and despised him. He sat at the head of the table, bloated and broken-veined, fooling with a waitress and then asking for expensive dessert wines in a suddenly serious voice. It was time to leave, if only to dodge my way artfully back to the Crypto-Amnesia or sit in a plastic armchair at some small hotel and drink warm gin and tonic.

There was a power of sorts in this collection of people surrounded by flowers and glasses and ashtrays, but it was a strange power. Within this arch calm, it seemed as though a crisis was being manufactured, ready to jostle itself into the history books of the future. 'How We Astroturfed Arcadia', a brief summary by Mr Ex, to rhyme with hex, meaning 'out of', as in 'whore de combat', or 'whore d'oeuvres'. Archer's party minus Lisa was a bordello beyond boredom, the cat house at the end of the world, and we were all generating the loneliness of prostitutes. We were being paid off for services rendered with this ritual of mutual dedication.

Amelia looked ill. She was finding the boredom physically corrosive. The atmosphere was wearing away her bodily outline, the strata of tedium gradually widening like glacial chasms across her chest. Soon there would simply be a trail of remains left in the bore-hole that used to be her body — an echo of conversation perhaps, a black bra and an earring, the rest of her quite dissolved in the plasma of dullness that had enveloped her during the sorbet.

It was definitely time to leave. It had been an anti-climax. No rescue. I took what was left of Amelia's hand and led her quietly to where Archer sat. We thanked him very much indeed for the lovely evening and made arrangements to meet soon which none of us had the slightest intention of keeping.

As we left the restaurant, I looked back over my shoulder at the party in the distance; an altar shrouded with smoke.

'Where shall we go?' We took deep breaths on the deserted pavement.

'The Crypto-Amnesia?' I suggested.

'Are you mad?' replied Amelia. 'Look at the sky — it's too dark to go to the Crypto-Amnesia, it wouldn't even be safe . . .' A jest. Black shapes were moving around beneath the moon. We lounged against the window of a second-hand bookshop, feeling lost. We didn't want to part just yet. We both wanted to carry on.

'I know,' said Amelia, 'we'll go and visit Helen. She'll tell us what to do, she'll know . . .'

Another taxi, a flare of matches, another address, somewhere near Limehouse. I watched Amelia trying to lower the window as we drove off, and then I turned away. Neither of us spoke.

THIRTEEN

Chemicals, Islands, and Mud

Helen Smith was proud of her eyes. It was more than mere vanity over their beauty. She had never met, or seen anywhere, a person with eyes the same colour as hers. Her eyes were purple, the colour of lilac in full bloom. As a teenager, watching the snow slowly whiten her parents' garden, Helen had been aware that she saw the world through extraordinary purple eyes. She had despised her first boyfriend as the light off the snow was embalming his face in the dusk. She had studied the irises in the vase on her mantelpiece as she told him that she never wanted to see him again. She had been quite impersonal about it, admiring, as she spoke, the discipline and poise with which the delicate heads of the flowers were supported on the vicious, straight foils of their stems.

In the seven years since then there had been men, many of them, seldom getting close to her but always trying. The few who had come within grazing distance had always reached out to stroke her cheek, or her forehead, or neck, and then fallen into the trap of her eyes. She had watched men drown in her eyes. At times like these, as she looked at the men flailing around hopelessly before her, her eyes deepened even further. Through tears or anger her eyes took on the liquid brilliance of freezing methylated spirits. In the aftermath of her suitor's heated departure she would study her cold expression in the mirror. Her eyes shone like amethysts in acid. The men had all desired her eyes, or the qualities of love that they assumed her eyes suggested, and this jealous coveting of the feature that she held most dear had rendered her wary. The wariness had gradually turned into hatred, the hatred had worn itself out during the long bleak winters of her adolescence, and finally, as the late frosts sculpted her into a tall, boyish beauty, she had forgone all public emotion concerning her attitudes. It remained a question of chemicals, however, the matter of her eyes; the certainty of formula.

Now Helen's beautiful eyes looked out on nothing, as I discovered the evening that Amelia and I went to visit her, and the reason for this went back, I suppose, to the day when Helen was walking down the damp-blackened path across Grosvenor Square as the leaden autumn air was chilling out to offend the ambassadorial atmosphere of Mayfair. That morning her hands had felt as thin as paper; brittle, inflammable things that could hardly hold her mascara. During the day an inner vacancy had taken possession of her, spreading out so fully inside her head as to be almost too large for the physical confines of her skull. She was terrified by its completeness. As opposed to accepting the sensations that her surroundings injected into her, she was left weightless by the manner in which her vacancy, her poltergeist, excluded all feeling on contact. She owned no sensations.

The vacancy ran on ahead of her as she walked; she could no longer anticipate the streets beyond, the turning of the misty corner, the yellow lights in the Connaught Hotel. There were no annexes, however subliminal and obscure, that she could explore in her imagination as she walked through her immediate tenancy of the moment. Helen was evicted from her body; she was a street walker, no fixed address.

It was getting darker, and the sky appeared to be lowering itself like a weatherbeaten sail to eclipse what little light was left in the square. Helen looked up to the trees, their black branches sticking out at rigid angles to dissect the corners of her vision with their worrying, glistening shapes. They were locked with nerves, or cramped into place by some foul rigormortis. The yellowing leaves hung limply down, no longer reminiscent of the sweet dampness that fills an orchard, but simply looking damp and ill — dying before their time.

Where was the Indian Summer? The city was swollen to a pulp on cold water. There could be no view, from any window, however high, that would welcome her eyes with a clear September sky that the dignity of the year's late middle age inscribed in a gentle curve of reddening clouds. There was nothing in the whole of London that was not swollen to corpulence in tune with her damp becoming frozen.

Everything seemed beyond her control. Helen's frozen purple eyes, deadly with beauty, were visiting her mood upon the city as surely as if she was casting spells. If she could gaze this fetid magic, then her own fate was written into the power: her eyes had reversible vision, seeing both the mute wax dome of the sky, and deep into her soul. She had the power of being a victim, an horrific twist of character now that everything looked the same, both within her and outside her.

As the fluid magic of this process washed in and out of her wonderful eyes, Helen grew weaker. She thought soon she would leave us, a beautiful Faustus, illiterate in sorcery and working miracles of bad magic upon herself by accident. The cold black sea of London would close up over her head and she would swim beneath its surface forever, twisting and turning in the darkness. She would stretch her long white arms up to the limit of their reach, clasping her hands above her when she could reach no further, and then be spiralled down to the depths of zero visibility, defying blindness with the saddest act of complicity — to gently close her purple eyes for the very last time and feel the soft curves of her black eyelashes coming to rest on her cheek, the pressure squeezing out the one hot tear she had left, a burning fleck of her life cast adrift into the smother of the freezing water.

She stood before her window in the early evening, unable to get warm. She ran a deep bath, slipping herself slowly into the water. In the hot water her body glowed an ugly red. She disliked the way her pale skin took the heat; she was proud of her white skin and short black hair and avoided any public disturbance of their effective combination which set off her eyes so well. In the privacy of her bath she stretched out in the bed of hot water, feeling the tightness in her head relax, letting the knots that trussed up her vacancy dissolve like biodegradable stitches. But binding what, or which, wound? The trends of her life endorsed the need for bandages but these could do nothing to cure the bad blood that flowed beneath them. Her wounds were open twenty-four hours — they never closed.

In her hands she pictured the hands of her last lover. She had never thought his hands were used to violence until the night he hit her. She had known him only a few days before that hideous night in Berkeley Square, and then she found herself in casualty, aware of the sordid story that her cuts and bruises shouted out as she haemorrhaged misinformation into the curious eyes of the onlookers. The doctor had avoided her eyes as he painted over the cuts with a thin, cruel antiseptic. Since that night, six months ago, she had been unable to get warm, hating all she saw. She still remembered the walk across the hospital car park, could still feel the heavy white powder she had dusted all over her swollen face, the sickly sweet taste of it on her cigarette, her lips.

Nowadays she could always sense a needle; some hypodermic dripping painkiller through her tensed, vein swollen arm. Waiting for the brutal injection to be performed by some bored assistant, a bureaucrat from the administration of arbitrary circumstances, the Final Symposium.

The man who had beaten her was now a scorpion in her

pocket, a thing that lashed out and bit when she was looking for change. All she could remember of him was that he used first names like punishments.

She dried her hair and did her eyes, returning to the open window. She could feel the mist filling her nostrils with its odour of dead candles, blown all the way from Southwark, she could almost taste the sea. There was a scratch of saline moisture down the oyster pearl of her lipstick. If she were to fly low down the river that night, in a helicopter, down beyond the Isle of Dogs, with a searchlight running on ahead, a sunspot on the water, sooner or later she would be looking at nothing but furrows of grey estuary silt, striped like a zebra skin chair, and running out into the ocean.

There are certain states of mind that expand with time like monotonous suburbs around a central citadel of indecision. Helen was living in the hinterland of such a state in those days, her diaphanous purple eyes casting worried glances to the horizon. She stared through London with a vitreous humour. She craved warmth. Looking into the power station night she shivered at the cold winds that blew there. She had longed for a white wedding at Christmas when young.

Her eyes were icing over, virtually blinding her. Her conversation jittered, the words refusing to lie flat.

Out of the past came Amelia, a childhood and teenage friend. She decided to write to her, the last ditch.

It was months since she had written anything, and her hands held the pen like a stick. She felt as though she was scratching her name on the low tide mud, a temporary monument. She could not form the sentences at first, she became the author of babble, an illegible scrawl. She kept the scrawl.

Helen lay on the floor all night, a candle beside her flickering across the carpet. Finally she had written the letter:

So I am writing to you now Amelia, it is me, Helen, you

must remember Helen.

It is the story of the eyes Amelia. I haven't been out much but now they are playing some music over the river and I can hear it, buzzing in at my window like poor Tinkerbell.

I think I now know, Amelia. Do you know what it's like to know? Have you got that stupid feeling too? Do you feel like a chemistry set? I am a weak gymnast at times like this, Amelia, synonymous with depressed dilettante and I bet you know all about that. And I bet you know too, that without love the most passionate mood to cross the day is a war between pornography and poetry with you as a celibate hostage on both sides. Stupid stupid. If I had a glass house now I'd throw flowers in it. I don't make sense.

So after we're dead what? A symposium perhaps? Can I really come alive on paper Amelia? Or even be convincingly dead? Marks in black ink — I do not think their sense is permanent anyway. Do you suppose that words deteriorate Amelia? The more we use them? The easier we use them? To know something anyway, the way it looks.

The city is dead tonight, but I am not to blame for that. It is drowned and drunk and damaged and dead. I am cold. So here is the tarty ribbon to tie on the framed edition of my feelings Amelia, you idiot, you take it.

But Helen did not send this letter to Amelia for some months, at least, not until she had returned from Italy, which is where she went, to sort-herself-out as they say.

Not merely content to pass beyond the Isle of Dogs, Helen went south to Venice, soon to find herself widening her eyes experimentally to the warm air that drifted across the lagoon as she sat alone with her driver in a taxi cutting the black water to the city.

It was dusk, and in the jeweller's velvet of the sky a thousand stars were shining. She felt the massive distance that she had travelled from the clammy edges of the London autumn. She could imagine a host of salt water ghosts rising up from the sea around her, things whose kisses would drag the feminine city to its knees with desire. The passion play chimed in the air, its desires as secular and erotic as its intentions were mystical.

Each day broke over her like a low chord. Taking the boat to Torcello, she passed the peaceful walled island of San Michele. It sat so low in the water, the Venetian dead lying at rest among the scorched evergreens, their lives ended with the greatest paradox, to be landlocked for eternity in the middle of the sea.

Helen leant on the warm steel rail of the ship, watching the rhythmic passage of the waves. Her arm would tan if she stayed there too long, but only up to the elbow. She shifted her stance, resting her head against the galley door. The sea rose up to the white horizon, hemstitched invisibly into the sky.

She pulled a loose tress of hair down in front of her eyes and looked at it closely. Raven black. It had been a whim to sit in a window high above the Grand Canal and let a stranger cut her hair. The light had come in across her face and so she had closed her eyes. Her face was half in shadow then, the wall behind obscured with sun. The tall window frames were rotten, the thick panes of glass coming loose in their putty — she had been in love with the window frames.

For an instant, a freshening breeze. At Torcello there were miles and miles of charred scrub, a church tower rising up out of the embers. A locked church, a blistering tow path.

In the salt grass crackling to splints and tinder she watched a black butterfly dipping from flower to flower, the only sign of life. She stood alone on the hot island, motionless in her cement white dress. Helen wanted something to rise from the dead grass and take her away with it.

Of course, nothing did, but from that moment on she felt that somehow the back of her crisis had broken, that the chicane of acute nervousness which she had found herself being squeezed through was finally widening into a straighter

— if more commonplace — stretch of existence.

On her return to London, Helen immersed herself in a social life, apparently coming to the Crypto-Amnesia Club three nights out of five. I never met her there. I cannot be expected to have met everyone who comes to my club.

Amelia told me Helen's story. Helen was her friend.

FOURTEEN

A Visit to Helen Back

Already in possession of the mythological portrait of Helen that Amelia had passed on to me, I was at a loss to know quite what to expect that spring night when we pulled up beside her flat. As if Heaven had walked on Earth? No. You walk down a cinder path to get to where she lives. The cinders glow red in the street light. Helen has a nickname: she is called 'The Badger'. This was due to her passionate involvement with the ska music revival in the late seventies, before her disappearance, and it is this public identity which has immortalised itself in her sobriquet. She used to be seen at night wearing a big parka anorak that reached down to her knees. One night she got some black and white paints and wrote on the back of it: 'THE BADGER SE5'.

Helen lives near the river, seldom venturing out these days, but it is rumoured that she is writing a gangster novel, the prose rhythms of which are inspired by Prince Buster. No one really knows for sure however, and I am more inclined to believe Amelia when she says that Helen just sits around listening to records and feeling emotionally unattractive. I don't think that I have ever encountered someone as bitter — in a deep down, rooted kind of way — as Helen.

We stopped by the river wall on our way down the cinder path, just to take the obligatory look at the water. There was a lot of wreckage and mess down there in the mud — signed record sleeves, fold-out poster magazines, hotel bedroom keys, menus. We moved off again in silence, exhaling clouds of frozen breath and looking up at the hideous block that Helen lived in, bronze beneath the sky, and sweating slightly. Amelia was humming something as we walked up the path. The whole visit was clammy. I wanted to go to sleep, or back to the office. A wind came up off the river, whistling over the stacks of old bottles that stood outside the door. Aeolian garbage, a soundtrack to the domestic arguments that were floating down from the over-heated kitchenettes in the darkness high above us.

The block of flats was long, and tall, and barnlike. In places it glowed a flesh colour, the black fire-escapes clamping the walls together like the ectoskeleton of some horrible brick insect. On the stairs the time switch was broken, so we walked up in the dark. I tried to note the number of stairs in case I ever had to run down them sometime, but got bored and simply plodded on behind Amelia. There were long windows stretching the height of the building, the staircase marking time with them, fastened with a sticky red bannister that gleamed nastily like some internal organ. Through the dirt on the windows you could see the river: a line of black and white with crimson smudges where the lights were. The central core of the lift cage followed us up on the other side. It was broken. A dull orange light brooded in the black pit at the bottom of the open shaft. God knows what it was — it moved around a bit, and sighed. The red lights that hung on the outside of the building at each landing cast at regular intervals a murderous glow over the concrete steps. They left a mark as if a body had just been dragged away. The little oblong landings all had damp black stains in the corners. Everywhere smelt of gas and disinfectant.

We pushed on through the darkness. 'What makes you think that Helen is going to be in?' I said, 'and what makes you think that if she is she'll want to see us?' There was a pause in the footsteps above me and then a voice floated down, 'Have you got any better ideas?' I had no ideas at all, so we carried on climbing.

Helen greeted us without enthusiasm. She was wearing a black dress and a pair of dark glasses. 'Why have you come round?'

Amelia threw her scarlet overcoat onto a sofa and looked uneasy. 'We just thought that we'd come and see you . . .'

'This is stupid,' I said. There were drawings on the wall. A Christ, and a Road-Block.

'Would you like a drink?' muttered Helen, snapping off a soundless television and disappearing into her little kitchen.

'Yes' we replied, stuck for an answer.

'Well what would you like? I've got coffee-style hot drink and tea-style hot drink. And some white port.'

'Tea.'

'Port.'

'Alright.'

Amelia and I sat at opposite ends of the sofa, our hands on our knees, staring dead ahead. An old dansette record player was open in one corner, a stack of records beside it. Reggae, Blue Note. Helen came back carrying three teacups, two of which contained tea, the third white port. She knelt beside her record player, looking for a record to play. 'We didn't come here to play records,' said Amelia, annoyed at the deadpan way Helen seemed to be manipulating the situation into one that it would be useless to continue.

'So where have you been tonight?' asked Helen, raising an eyebrow and taking a sip of tea, carefully avoiding our eyes as she swallowed it.

'We've been to a ghastly dinner party,' said Amelia, grasping at conversation eagerly.

'Whose?' asked Helen.

'It was Archer . . .' Amelia's words tailed off at the look that Helen gave her. The subject was dropped.

'And who's he?' said Helen, meaning me.

'I'm the man-with-no-theories,' I said, meaning 'It doesn't matter.'

'Smart,' replied Helen, meaning 'moron.'

The visit was dying. Then again, there was no reason for us to be there. It had been an impulse. The fact that Helen was not well disposed to anyone who was a friend of her assailant did not help matters. That had been the real kiss of death.

Getting up to leave, I asked Helen if she knew Lisa from Phone Cell. 'I thought everyone knew everyone at The Crypto-Amnesia Club,' she replied, with heavy sarcasm.

'So it seems,' I replied.

Standing outside on the cinder path again, I looked at Amelia.

'I wonder why she changed her name to Helen Back,' said Amelia.

'It doesn't take much working out,' I replied, 'and she does have the hallmark of a true club member . . .'

'The dark glasses?'

'No. Not really.'

The pointless visit had proved to me that Amelia and I had spent a long time going nowhere. The destination had always been vague anyway. I hadn't really ever left The Crypto-Amnesia Club, where everyone knows where to find everyone else by the debris they leave behind them. I liked Amelia anyway.

FIFTEEN

Hard Women In Jersey Dresses

As a missing suspect Lisa renders my interrogation of the past most difficult to continue. Maybe she knows that I am lost, looking for a clue — or at least a motive — as to why I feel this way. She can't supply one. I think that her anticipation of this drove her away. It made her ill. After the pointless visit to Helen Back's, things dragged on exhaustingly and I remained as uncertain of my real needs as ever. I was backwards pioneering I suppose, returning from the wilderness to try and find out what it was in civilization that drove me away from it. I could draw a map only in retrospective terms, plotting the contours of a massive nostalgia with the inaccuracy of detail that was inevitable when left to a numb-fingered cartographer such as myself. At best it was a drag-footed meander across a dark swamp of contradictions, obscured with marsh gas, and peppered with emotional sparks that set off random flares in the mist.

And then I received an envelope, post-marked Brussels, and addressed in Lisa's writing. From its contents I managed to piece together something of what Lisa had been doing. After she had left me she left London and went to Belgium. To a small suburb to the south of Brussels, an indistinct and anonymous suburb off the motorway that leads to Leuven. She didn't look anything like her passport photograph anymore. She had grown her hair and dyed it so blonde as to be almost white. Her face was thinner, her eyes defined only by the black waxy pencil that she drew around them. Her lips were pale and bloodless, the backs of her hands scarred by the nervous lacerations she continually inflicted on herself with her long brittle nails. So much she described to me.

She weathered the cold spring in three grey rooms, with a grey gasfire that dried out the air and a balcony whose door wouldn't open. She lived on the sick pay that Phone Cell advanced to her, more out of pity than anything else, but I suspect that she was given some stupid honorary title such as European Rep, or some such nonsense. She passed the time taking photographs, hundreds of them. Drunken tourist snapshots that cut things in half and let in too much light or no light at all. I think that she actually saw the landscape the way that these bad photographs revealed it. She must have sat on the rug in front of her gasfire night after night, trying to make sense of all those bad photographs, but why? Looking for traces of a latent talent on which she could build a new life? Reminding herself that she was still alive? I don't know. In this, as in nearly everything else between us, there is no such thing as a tangible reason.

There had always been flashes of brilliance across Lisa's small talent for the unusual, these moments inspired by her painful witnessing of scenes that reminded her of some essence or other, some representative glimpse. The rest of the time she put on an act, an act which every so often was impossible to keep up. The Brussels interlude was one of her lapsed periods, and it must have been a wretched life. I hesitate to reconstruct it here, based on so much dubious guesswork and so few facts, but there is some cruel streak in me that drives me to describe it. Perhaps I fantasize over the partially hidden.

I imagine the moon, rising full over Brussels, tangled in the treetops above a little square. The crystal glass in front of Lisa still holds a drop of crème de menthe. Like a mouthful of grass somehow, but for once it has been a clear day in Brussels, and this has inspired in her the confidence to mimic the fiesta drinks of summer. For one day at least, Lisa has been able to assume from the clearer sky and the softer air that the Lion is finally out, and that one can henceforth anticipate kinder treatment from the Lamb. By late afternoon, as the windows were glowing in the office buildings, she had been reminded of Brighton — or Marseilles — some slab of vanilla ice cream that kept its shape beneath the deep blue sky.

Alone in the café, early evening, the cold comes down again, intensified by the clear sky. Lisa is a chain, a silver chain, from London to the crystal to the moon, her stomach a mess of art-nouveau and the chill burning her fingers with its invisible blue fishtail. She is smoking Tigers which come in flat packs of twenty-five. Her cheap camera is on the table beside her, and she is scrawling postcards in a wavering, childish hand, before slipping them all into one brown envelope, already addressed. And this was the envelope that I received, bulging with cards and photographs.

She writes: 'Dethmobile,' only to cross it out again. Then: 'It has been a lovely day today. How has it been with you?'

On a new card (a gaudy colour postcard of the Grande Place, all decked out for pageantry and tinted with airbrush), she writes: 'SCUMCLUB BURN/WHY ME? In our useless Baltic Sea I want a warm current. Sailing boats will be useless anyway. Useless at home. I have been splashing around in the shallows, there is always a cloud of insects above the rusty water.'

This? From Lisa? Why not?

The longest of these notes is written on two sheets of hotel notepaper, fastened to a pair of blurred photographs. One of the photographs I recognized as the steps leading up to the Place Rogier. The other is too out of focus; a park perhaps, or a zoo, but then there is a streak of gold running across it and a black shape down the left hand side. This picture is painful to look at, despite its hidden subject, and it is the pain somehow that makes me write this. The sheets are headed 'Hotel Simon Besac, Rue de Laeken, Bruxelles 1012.' There is no date. The handwriting is the same slow scrawl of schoolgirl precise. Black biro. She writes:

It's become impossible to talk to you. We always run out of things to say. I don't know if it's me or you. I always wonder whether I'm saying the right thing, or whether I've offended you. It's stupid.

Maybe we're bored with each other, but I don't know. I think maybe I'm not not saying the things that you want me to say, and all that means is that I'm not the person you thought I was. You've got the wrong girl.

Nothing flows between us anymore. It's painful to be together. My eyes are strained from the feeling that something's wrong.

The Botanical Gardens were red today. I missed you. It rained again.

I would like to talk to you but can't anymore. All the talk bottled up inside me is making me sick. I just seem to describe things to myself, you know, things that describe themselves. I comment on the obvious to fill my mind. It's the job I've set myself. It's pointless, there's no reason for it, and without reasons things are pointless, because there is no action, and without action there is nothing for us to talk about. You always said that my mistake was movement. You were wrong.

I think that my stupid job and your stupid club were the things that made me unhappy. And I loved you except it all went wrong. It might have worked.

The rest is missing. I can only guess, but it's pretty obvious. I find myself dragged into thinking of her life in Brussels, if only to feel close to her. I see her in my mind, but like she used to be, on a Friday morning perhaps, looking for magazines at a newsagents on the rue Neuve. She is deep in thought as she chooses which to buy. She can smell the shrinkwrapping and the stationery. She is looking at the slabs of Italian and French magazines: L'Officiel, Donna, Casa Vogue, Vogue Bambini, Gap, Elle, Uomo Monde, Vogue Italia, Lei, Vogue Pelle, Linea Uomo, and Marie Claire.

'Which shall, which shall, which shall I buy?' she thinks, as her hands and heart and eyes race one another down the racks. Out of the corner of her eye she can see other people, also buying magazines. What could be more ordinary than a girl shopping for magazines?

A girl shopping, as natural as breathing. She would buy five magazines, pay, and walk out, the glass doors swishing shut behind her.

Outside, the air suddenly troubles her. It snags once at her breath, a nervous jerk. She clears her throat, and then looks down the street. She heads towards the Galerie Ansbach, knowing that department stores soothe. She will buy some tights. Premier Etage: Lingerie. Still troubled, she walks quickly to the store, bumping into people. She becomes aware of where she is, a growing sense of horror coming from the realisation that she alone is responsible for guiding herself down the street, into the store, up the escalator, to the counter, to choose the tights, pay the girl, leave, walk out and breathe . . . But then what?

A street vendor is selling mechanical toys. Pink dogs and blue cats. They won't keep still. They play little drums and smash together little cymbals. She can't look at them. Insane and self-possessed, these toy animals rotate with fixed stares in the stolen supermarket trolley that they call home.

Lisa feels as though she's dying. Her breath comes in gasps as she pushed her way through the crowd of hard women in jersey dresses who window shop along the street.

She heads down an alley towards the Grande Place, hoping that maybe among the solid civic buildings she will feel the steadying hand of a father. She slows down, dazed and confused, then somehow wanders into a little shop that sells pommes frites and cans of drink. There is a short, Latin man, dressed in greasy white overalls, waiting behind the counter. He has eyes like slits of rubber and no neck.

'Freeeetes mademoiselle?' he leers, bending over his metal baskets as the frites sizzle in the boiling fat.

'Merci,' she gasps.

The chip man of Brussels looks up at her with a knowing wink. He smiles, showing his teeth which are blackened like a geisha courtesan's. Into the paper cone they slide, the long hot glistening frites, and then he says, 'MAYONNAISE MADEMOISELLE?'

She *still* wakes screaming when she recalls his face.

Maybe it was something like that which drove Lisa back to her three room hide-out to look at photographs night after night, as the rain fell steadily over the suburbs and the leaves of the plants on her balcony dripped endlessly through the long evenings. An overhead light and a sense of doubt . . .

Brussels was the last place I had expected her to be.

SIXTEEN

'Nor Saw the Towers of Troy'

The weeks pass by, each weekend leaving a kind of tide mark on the days. No one really believes in the weekend, it's just an horizon to pull for, and we all seem to do it. Perhaps we are all traditional and conservative at heart, all lounge bars with crimson flock and perspex mahogany, wherever we choose to drink.

As I sit in the office, drumming my fingers on the desk top or tracing the course of a tropical fish with my face hard against the glass, I always return to Lisa's envelope. It is lying in the middle of my desk, and I search for new interpretations of my life among its contents. The envelope is my candle in the window, my scholar's thesaurus. It is an envelope full of cards and photographs. It helps me to pass the time. It looks grey under the dim blue lights in the office, and when Sydney comes in to discuss policy or settle the accounts I always find my hand straying towards it, stroking it like a sacred bone as Amphe yawns in my face.

Time was passing by like this, each day leaving me more certain that if only I could break some code within the envelope I would find revealed a secret message from Lisa to myself, something that could only be for our mutual good. I acted out heroic scenarios in my head, sometimes miming the deeds to myself, a method actor in a problem play.

And then, one night, a Thursday, the light on my telephone

began to wink. I looked at it warily.

'Hello.'

'Hello Boss, Lisa's outside . . .'

'. . . ! . . .'

'It's Lisa — from Phone Cell. Shall I show her in . . .?'

'. . . ? . . .'

'You alright Mr Merril? It's LISA . . .'

'Why?'

'Sorry Boss?'

'Show her in . . .'

I stood up behind my desk, gently resting my hands on its surface. This was the moment I had been thinking about for months. This was the moment I had been describing to myself for so long that what I was describing no longer had anything to do with this moment. In the tradition of such moments, it seemed to me as though nothing happened for a very long time, and I picked up the phone just to check that I hadn't been hearing things. I looked around the office curiously. I looked at my watch. 11.45. Then I heard vague noises outside the door, and already I could tell from their unique quality of expensive rustling and a low giggle that it could only be Lisa. The door was pushed open, admitting a blast of white light and a noise that made me jump back a step and put my arm over my eyes. Fumbling for my dark glasses I blinked at the scene before me. There was Sydney, all Top Man executive and a wry smile, and there was another man, far better dressed than Sydney and almost as tall. He was wearing an expensive charcoal grey suit and a crimson tie. A vague, stupid grin fought past my better judgement and crawled onto my face.

'How do you . . .'

'Merril! . . . Darling! . . .'

The voice had come from nowhere. Then, bursting through the two men in the doorway came Lisa, fresh faced, radiant, her blonde hair swept up into a luxurious mass on top of her head. There was a wide strip of vermilion where her mouth was and her entire body was wrapped up in yards of black silk and fine netting. On her throat there was an immense necklace of unashamed diamonds, each stone cascading a milky white light.

I suddenly sneezed, and Amphe shot off my desk and curled around the feet of the man who was accompanying Lisa.

'Why . . . Lisa! How lovely to see you. I was wondering if you'd ever come and pay us all a visit . . .'

Even as I spoke my stomach was churning. The kiss that I had dreamt myself to sleep with at my desk so many times was over before I knew it had happened.

'Merril. I had to tell you first . . . because you're my very best, most special, oldest, friend . . .'

The grin, by now entirely autonomous, had widened to ghastly proportions across my face.

'Uh huh?'

Lisa sat down with a sound like an ice cap breaking up and crossed her legs with a jaunty, continental confidence. I sat down. I felt more in control sitting behind my desk. The strange man came and stood like a perfect gentleman behind Lisa's chair, leaning forward with a scarcely perceptible bow to light her cigarette with a slim black lighter which gave a smart electronic click as it pouted its little kiss of flame.

'I've got so much to tell you Merril . . . but we must have lunch . . . I've heard that there's this fabulous new restaurant called Short Hemline . . .'

'Well, I wouldn't say it's that . . .'

'. . . and we really must go, just the two of us, and discuss old ti . . .'

'Who's your friend?'

Lisa flashed a knowing smile across her bare shoulder to the towering stranger. The stranger, obviously in on the language, smiled back. I glared into the middle distance and then managed to drag the grin back just in the nick of time.

'Well this . . .' (gesturing at the man with a triumphant

giggle that made her coiffure tremble slightly) 'as you've probably guessed, is the best part of my news Merril. This . . . is André . . . my husband.'

'Enchanté, M. Merril.'

It spoke! Like a drugged king singing his own death warrant as the revolutionary committee crowded around the throne, I shook hands. I could feel his warm, expensive skin touching my clammy, thin, palm.

The room did not sway, or light up in a blaze of colour. Nothing.

'How do you do,' I replied, too naturally. 'Congratulations!' I shouted this.

There was something so obviously protective in André's bodily positioning of himself around Lisa. He was like a high wire fence. I gestured with a laugh to the envelope on my desk. 'I was just getting around to looking at all . . .'

Lisa shot me a violent glance. The envelope was obviously taboo. 'Oh those!' she trilled with a pretty sneer, 'so they finally reached you then . . . I'd more or less forgotten about them . . .'

'Well, I rather wondered whether anything was wrong . . . I mean going from these . . .' My voice trailed off into a hoarse whisper. I lit a cigarette, noticing André wince slightly at the odour of Virginia tobacco.

'Oh God, you know me darling,' said Lisa, 'ups and downs, ups and downs; but now I've found my permanent up.' And she caressed André's besuited flank with all the care of a proud owner.

It was time for all this to end. I couldn't take them and their love anymore. I stood up, a broad beam plastered over my face.

'Well, I certainly am happy for you both,' I leered. 'Take good care of her André old chap! This girl's an old friend of mine!' I was going to be sick.

Lisa stood up, just slightly too quickly, and offered a perfectly powdered cheek which she kept just out of reach of the traditional peck. My lips merely brushed her face, clumsily.

'Well remember our lunch Merril, that's a date!' (All said with a playful daring irony that was the ultimate in castration technique.)

'A pleasure M. Merril,' said André, offering his hand again. 'I am so glad to meet the manager of the chic "Creepto Amnesia Club", although I must say I am glad that Lisa no longer needs to work here . . .'

'She never did work h . . .'

'There seemed to be some trouble as we were . . .' He tactfully cut short his concern, a broad smile breaking out on his suntan.

Insincere goodbyes all round. Lisa and André swept out through the Phone Bar like Oberon and Titania leaving the Cannes Film Festival.

As I walked slowly back to the office that no longer held any treasure, I caught a glimpse of some overdressed brat prancing around with an icebucket on his head and stumbling into groups of innocent bystanders. I summoned Sydney.

'Get that moron out of here,' I snapped. 'Why are there so many fucking idiots in here tonight?' And without waiting for an answer I strode back into the office and slammed the door, letting out the last of Lisa's perfume. Lisa had found her common market.

SEVENTEEN

Mirage

Lisa and André seemed to stay floating in my office for days. I sat behind the desk, a rabbit stunned in the headlights, and every time I closed my eyes I saw, in greater detail, the scene that had taken place between us. I blinked and saw the pale blue powder around her eyes, I blinked again and saw his strong hand resting softly on her shoulder. With each blink, with each pause for thought, a more harrowing glimpse of our conversation passed before my eyes.

It was, I knew, more trouble than it was worth. My pity had not her grace obtained, and all that was proven from the whole affair was that when dealing with Lisa you could be certain of no certainties.

There I was, a man alone on burning sands where nothing has ever been known to happen, kicking at the dunes with a bitter laugh: 'Least I've got a desert.'

That so much could be wiped out so quickly, leaving nothing but this. I find it hard that the prose versions of our lives — all short cuts and ruthless practicalities — can so easily oust the poetry that we have striven to come to terms with during interminable stretches of solitary confinement. Somewhere in the back of my mind various things were happening of their own accord; random, inconsequential thoughts, that defied the call of reason and simply left a sick regurgitated taste in the battered old wardrobe that I call a mind. There was a mental image of Hampton Court Maze in July (sunny), and the sound of a feeble, tired, voice singing 'I Can't Give You Anything But Love (Baby),' to a slurred accordion accompaniment.

With the desertion of my heroics, I felt myself to be lying down in the middle of the floor to receive a dose of the slapsticks, and this gradual crumpling of myself into an emotional underlay for Lisa and André's magic carpet gave me great distress. It was a question of finding some strength again.

It is surprising how very alone you can be left in the heart of a night club. It helps if you own it. I was only just beginning to discover how secure I had made my retreat at The Crypto-Amnesia Club, and I began to look at it with new eyes, trying to assess what exactly — if anything — it stood for. It stood for failure, obviously, and for a subtle kind of failure that looked very similar to success. There were two hundred Lisas out there on weekday nights alone, twice that number on Saturdays; tarted up Rhine Maidens who slum it nights, and whirl remorselessly around the eye of the storm, all shoes, and eyes, and neck. Nothing really worked at The Crypto-Amnesia Club — least of all the guests — except the technology. People just became puppets who could sling back a drink or affect a new attitude without getting too tangled in their strings. The Crypto-Amnesia provides the philosophical lubricant that allows falsehood to pass as truth — with just a wink and a tip to the doorman.

If Lisa seemed to me to be a lover — the lover — who could grant a purpose to my life then I begin to believe that anyone else who is pretty enough can do the job just as well; that is, not do anything at all.

As regards all the love letters I have written to Lisa but never sent, I may as well get them all photocopied now, just to have enough for the saturation leafleting.

I morbidly took to describing Lisa and André's affair to myself; mimicking their voices in my head, and imposing my own warped narrative onto their possible fortunes. I nailed a leather jacket onto the pristine wall of their dream home. I imagine:

'Well, as we've got an hour to kill, or maybe more, let's talk philosophy,' says Lisa.

She bribes André with a winning smile and then, 'Mmm. Let's,' he replies.

'Why is it?' she says.

'Why is it what?' he counters, the rogue!

'Why — oh, nothing. Why. I hate this conversation.' She turns, cat-like to the window, a dark window, heightened with gold.

'That's life,' dribbles André, pleased to score this Pyrrhic point.

'I thought you were my husband!' Lisa flings a look like an ashtray at him, her deadliest.

Silence.

'Then go!' she commands. He stays exactly where he is. Like history, he twists in his seat, and waits.

A minute and a half pass like a gimmick. 'Where shall we eat tonight?' she says.

'Where would you like to eat?' he counters like a benevolent despot. Lisa does not spot his hidden tyranny.

'At La Chimera darling pleeeese. Where they play the music loud.'

'It will only screw you up,' he answers, 'but have it your way. At the moment we are as free as air.'

'Why do you try to run my life?' Lisa asks with a sudden moodiness that is as inevitable as a sunset.

'Because you always try to literalise a metaphor.'

Lisa is impressed by this. 'Wow,' she says. 'Wow. Can we go to bed?'

'No,' he replies, finally certain of later pleasure. He thinks of her sucking a sexy ice cube, holding the little ice nude until it melts between her fingers, then licking. Grenadine lips. Tongue.

With André, I suspect that Lisa would be like a child, fingering her blonde tresses, putting her finger in her mouth, and kicking up a fuss at the naughty nursery tea when he refused her more jelly.

'We *are* a funny pair!' she would say to him over the Rum Fudge à Chimera Ice Cream Sorbet. André looks severe.

'That's because we understand one another Lisa.' (He opens up like a treasure chest.) 'Not content with the apathetic love that you are used to, I ensure that our feelings for each other are constantly on the move — up and down, before and behind.'

And Lisa feels the deepest admiration for him as he says these clever things.

And in my imagination I return to the Eats Lounge at the Chimera Club where the bill has just arrived, a tactfully folded square foot of hand made paper cast upon a reef of after-dinner chocolate shrimps.

'My God!' screams André. 'That's reasonable — we won't come here again.' And contemptuous of the whole affair he pays with real money.

They go out dancing next, to Continental Joe's. People sway across the floor like willow trees to the slow stuff, boys and girls more beautiful than the flowers of spring. They are among their own kind. To the full dance-mix of 'A Season In Hell with the Wrecking Crew' they leave, knowing themselves to be on the threshold of a memorable evening. (And as I sit here in my swivel chair it is all so clear to me now.)

'I have,' (André says, lying back in his speeding open-top sports car), 'I have had the most wonderful time.' He smiles. Her long blonde hair blows back with the wind into the blue dawn sky.

'Thank you for coming,' he says as they pull up by the dream house, the headlights catching the name on the door, 'Dream House'. Petrol fumes mingle with the scent of mown grass.

They kiss! Two beauties, two absolute little charmers.

They never row, or doubt; their love is simply piled on as it were by Fortune's silver tongs into their glass bonbonier. During the summer of their love, its fruits ripen to a sweet yellow weight . . . ready to drop. (And back in the dim blue office my eyes shine a bit.)

They go off on their perfect holiday, to Kenya perhaps, where at the scarlet dinner hour the palm leaves blow black in the window against the fiery tropical sky.

I imagine Lisa sitting in the bathroom of their bridal suite, the white vase beside her a fountain of local orchids. Leading off her dressing room there is a little bamboo door on to the veranda. The most expensive hotel in the sub-continent and still it could all go wrong. Remember Merril!

The water tumbles luxuriously into her bath, and her bath makes her happy — happier in fact than anything else; the bath would be the pinnacle of the whole experience somehow. André sits in a wide wicker chair, sipping a little dry vermouth, and watching pink birds fly over the jungle.

'Do not, do not, do not let us ever waken,' she suddenly says one day.

'Waken darling?' André replies — just a little too quickly — and then gently take her soft brown hand.

Lisa lets a designer tear fall perfectly. The tear comes — softly, beautifully even, from the corner of her left eye. It rises on the perfect crescent of her dark eyelashes, and then, retaining its exquisite contours, falls gracefully a half centi-metre onto the delicate powder of her cheek. With all the stately elegance of a princess entering a gala, the tear proceeds carefully down her face, etching a beautiful design as it trickles, but knowing exactly the right moment when to stop, evaporate, and disappear as if by magic.

Remember Merril!

God-like, André takes her other hand. 'What are you afraid off my darlingest darling?' he asks, like the moved hero that he is.

'Time,' she replies, with an abstract simplicity, before

rising to regret her foolishness and smile like one saved.

And several thousand miles away, Merril would be doing something inconsequential, like waiting for an antiquated lift to squeak up to him, and for the oversprung concertina door to shoot back on itself and admit him into the dowdy tortoiseshell light of its interior. Remember Merril . . .

And then what? Then they would return from their holiday to find the leaves blowing up the garden path to their dream house, and the perfect garden all overgrown in a tangle of rusty roses and wild mint. Then he says he has to go away on business — and the weeks begin to pass, and his business goes on and on.

She would sit surrounded by furniture draped in dust sheets and think of a gust of wind blowing the ash off a middle aged divorcee's cigarette, he's never around anymore. No more good fairies slide down the gathered silk pavilion that canopies their bed. Nobody comes to help. It's all gone wrong.

(But of course, it hasn't. And it never will. One look at the happy couple was enough to make me certain that they'll make old bones together.) But I can dream.

My imaginings of their love begin to unfold like fabric, suddenly changing in texture; their love contracts a sickness. They try washing under the arms of their love, but the tryst is rotten, and there is nothing left for them now save the searching of corners with a nervous eye, unable to find security when they share a room. Nothing but forced adoration and awful politeness. With winter, Lisa and André fight. Neither of them gives in, they both bite deeper. Blood is ugly on love's teeth, it is the tartar of despair, a black plaque. Remember Merril!

An unsupportive future spreads out ahead of them, the previous spring a burlesque already. She curls up at night, sentimental, wringing the hanky that he gave to her. She cries like a punctured oil drum. Love works its last trick, pulling the bleeding dove slowly out of the silk top hat. She thinks she hears bells. She uses sentimentality like tissues to block a broken window. He's gone. (I finally dispose of André in my daydream, tasting the dish cold as it were.)

So then she would not remember me. She would go for independence, which means she would go for anyone at all who wasn't me. After a year perhaps, she would cheer up, suddenly bursting with nervous joy and really ready to swing.

Taking about an hour to put her nail polish remover into her Jean B cosmetics cabinet above the marblesque basin, Lisa would suddenly feel as light as air, full of summertime and confidence.

And then there would be a party, a perfectly timed burst of activity which would begin with the purr of the telephone. She picks it up: — sudden shock! What if it's . . . him? Oh well. 'Why hi!' she says (it isn't him), 'God hi Janet wow yeah hello. So long since uh uh huhuh, well you know what it's like, you went through it all with Si . . . uh huh, not quite the same I know . . . uh huh . . . Sure! I'd love to, yeahh, uh huh, about eight. How many people will be there . . . uh huh . . . mmm, a real party eh? No. Just the thing, great, thanks, uh huh bi-ii,' ping. And spraying on something comfortable, she would go to her friend Janet's party which would be like a house warming only worse, but far more respectable than the riots they have at The Crypto-Amnesia Club.

And there she'd be sure to meet a 'guy'. The guy is called . . . Dwight Latimer, a well-known photographer's assistant and general young blood. He fancies her at once.

'Hi! I'm Mitch,' says Dwight, his usual opener.

'Hello,' smiles Lisa over her glass of sparkling white held at chin level. 'I'm Ninette.'

'Here alone?' he asks over the top of her head.

'I was invited alone,' she counter bluffs.

And three hours later they would wake up side by side in a whirlpool of Liberty print duvet cover and she would kneel like a figurine beside smug Dwight and cry like a frightened child.

That was the last of my fantasies about Lisa. There only remained for me to write her the letter, the one I had been saving for a moment like this. After that I could ask Amelia to the Club for dinner, or sell the Club, or do nothing at all. It doesn't really make much difference.

EIGHTEEN

Looking Back — Take One

The letter that I wrote to Lisa. The last letter. These things must be said. Beyond advice and away. Lose contact completely at last, in the end.

It's an effort. But really, there are no flattering circumstances in which to contextualise this letter, no long grass, no shadows and mist, no willow aslant a brook. It's all lies. I wrote:

Dear Lisa,

Well now you've gone and left me there's this — a savage contempt. Maybe together we wouldn't be strong enough to understand it. Maybe together it's easy to feel independent, and confident, lulled into a false contentment out of faith in the potential of love.

Even as lovers I don't know how close we were to the god — sometimes I think we scarcely worked out the dimensions of the temple. We spent too long sitting on the steps in the sunshine. God knows, it's stupid enough already, but now it seems (for I have obviously failed with you), now it seems right to study these things alone, to learn from the contempt that I feel.

I think that I know all the answers already — The Stupid

Shall Inherit the Earth, and occupy its territories with the complacent authority of the self-righteous.

Until the tension breaks (as I feel that one day soon it shall), our pre-history and our little decline and fall must be described with new words; words that work nights as resistance fighters. They must be the underground attack upon the existing administration.

And in the true romantic tradition of such things, these words are obviously complicit with the fact that their cause is futile and headed only for failure. Words as martyrs as ultimate witnesses. Surely it is the great romantic fantasy for the lover to be shot down for love in front of the beloved who rejected him? For this is the literature of fetish, a language of sex and violence. And these are romantic words that I am writing now, desirous of being tied down and forced — although they may pretend otherwise.

Here is my sado-masochistic language, and these words have willingly become victims, broken by an addiction to a vision, that vision being a map of London; a seductive topography of anxiety through which I retrace our footsteps.

These words are my goodbye to you, and their death is upon your head.

Merril.

NINETEEN

The Bluebell Wood

I had known that it was all over between us when, on a chance visit to her room, I had seen two little pairs of walkman headphones hanging up over her bed, as neat and as smug as sugar cupids on a wedding cake.

And that seems years ago. One, maybe two, it doesn't matter. Somehow times have changed.

On either side I feel my head to be supported by birdsong. A lorry drones off somewhere down the deserted dual-carriageway. It's summer.

Dragged down to the level of details, I wander about a menagerie of arbitrary tame thoughts, pausing occasionally out of horrified fascination or simply good manners. A concern with the rebuilding of a manor house, victim of bad wiring in 1936, now standing in its own grove of shadows, roses overtaking the glassless casements, and doves swinging in and out of the branches that overhang the roofless walls.

This mournful prettiness is typical of the canon of trained meditations that I now use to deaden the effect of certain other sights: the ripped and scratched stickers that cover the ceiling of a tube train, the getting soaked between nowhere much and anywhere in particular, the British Museum, Vaughan Williams, barely London, barely anywhere, a walk. The outlines are as dim as dusk by now.

Not that any of these things exist, nor any particular

clearings in any particular wood. There never was a charcoal burner, not anywhere here. There are, however, some people, some coarse, unrefined people, who take my brambles to be madness in quite the wrong sense. They suggest hard work. It was. It is. I smile over my drink in the Jubilee Bar. 'It makes as much sense as any of it does . . .'

Trying to support three, maybe four, outlooks in one apology for a mind. That's hard work.

Damn it to Hell, this is London. There's, oh, there's that thing about St James tube station that seemed to make a lot of sense, there's . . . chest pains, yes, and a particular way of looking up the hill from Blackfriars to St Paul's, there is all my lost property.

There are a million stories in the strangely dressed city, and none of them makes sense. It used to be a search, if not for truth then for some acceptable substitute.

I have little yellow marks between my fingers and a peculiar attitude towards women and work. 'Fuck work,' I say, 'that's the worst possible metaphor for anything.' And then my voice trails off, some deep self-consciousness simply running out at me like a motorbike down a badly lit street. Then that terrible silence, which is such a conspicuous avoidance of the issue. Like a doorstep kiss, the peck on the cheek, the fists hitting out at the nearest hard surface. Pain.

Then again, way beyond the overspill housing, is my problem with time, but Oh God, not that again. (A million times over I have told myself that there is nothing to worry about. That there's nothing in it. An empty canvas.)

I feel my . . . head . . . falling backwards into thin air as though I am stretching out in a swimming pool. I think about ordinary, decent people, of the kind I've never trusted, coming back from a walk in the botanical gardens. An airliner passes once every forty seconds over the long white spread of the tropical house, all that glass going gun metal blue against the yolk of the sun thrown into a stormy sky. A girl, gazing up, would say,

'I wonder where . . .?' and then give up, reaching for the sky, both legs intact and dreaming.

Turning again, turning to look fourteen miles southwards out of London, and then kind of shaking your head slowly across a projected semi-circle, that is, in fact, at its actual point on the horizon, some four or five miles across, looking out, or over, there, is the Bluebell Wood.

And it was full of bluebells when she first took me there, one evening, years ago. It was bursting with bluebells. She had been so excited to show the wood off to me, and I fell in love with it, all but fearful of vocalising my feelings lest they should prove not febrile enough. It became, eventually, a monument to all that I lost. It was synonymous with all that I lost.

But is the Bluebell Wood still there? People, I think, will be in it now, because there is a training centre for a bank close by, and people will walk there, in the evening. But it will not be the same, smelling of rain and candles. It cannot be the same. If it is the same, waiting for my girl and me to repossess it, only this time definitely in love, it still could not be the same, because we never were in love, not now, not then, not ever.

Instead then, I watch a person saying goodbye to their friend. I can talk about that. I can give that away. It isn't worth anything. I hate all that. All that unconnected, disorientating thinking that is impossible to follow.

I sit here alone, aware of a problem of re-centralising. I feel like a government office, pushed out into the country, based at Bluebell Wood. A country trading estate, all tarmac sliproads and Ealing comedies weather, becoming, years later, bored to tears, cursed wth inefficiency, and sent back to London in disgrace.

It is sunset in London, pink and gold. I think of her gold raffia sandal, still vivid in my mind, with her slim gold ankle above it.

Greengage trees, garden centres, the shuffle shuffle click of the slide carousel. So much to give up and forget about.

TWENTY

Looking Back — Take Two

Of course, the short version:

Dear Lisa,

Burn in hell you bitch.
I love you.

Merril.